W9-ABT-349

David leaned in close and kissed her. Softly and not too quickly. In front of the hospital where they both worked.

Mission or not, the idea of rumors circulating about him and Terri didn't bother him in the least.

Now all he had to do was come up with a plan for a stellar evening. This had to be different. Something special just for her. He wanted to give her an experience she'd never had, one that would leave her with fond memories, in case his assignment destroyed their friendship.

After everything she'd told him, the least he could do was show her what an amazing woman he saw when he looked at her. Pulling up the tide charts, he set to work figuring out the details. He would give her an evening she couldn't dismiss later as a tactic or trick, no matter how the case with her brother ended.

HER
UNDERCOVER
DEFENDER

USA TODAY Bestselling Authors

DEBRA WEBB
& REGAN BLACK

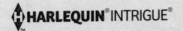

If you purchased this book without a cover you should be aware that this book is stolen property. It was reported as "unsold and destroyed" to the publisher, and neither the author nor the publisher has received any payment for this "stripped book."

With special thanks and love for Alysan,
who never stopped believing.

Recycling programs
for this product may
not exist in your area.

ISBN-13: 978-0-373-74923-2

Her Undercover Defender

Copyright © 2015 by Debra Webb

All rights reserved. Except for use in any review, the reproduction or utilization of this work in whole or in part in any form by any electronic, mechanical or other means, now known or hereinafter invented, including xerography, photocopying and recording, or in any information storage or retrieval system, is forbidden without the written permission of the publisher, Harlequin Enterprises Limited, 225 Duncan Mill Road, Don Mills, Ontario M3B 3K9, Canada.

This is a work of fiction. Names, characters, places and incidents are either the product of the author's imagination or are used fictitiously, and any resemblance to actual persons, living or dead, business establishments, events or locales is entirely coincidental.

This edition published by arrangement with Harlequin Books S.A.

For questions and comments about the quality of this book, please contact us at CustomerService@Harlequin.com.

® and TM are trademarks of Harlequin Enterprises Limited or its corporate affiliates. Trademarks indicated with ® are registered in the United States Patent and Trademark Office, the Canadian Intellectual Property Office and in other countries.

Printed in U.S.A.

www.Harlequin.com

Debra Webb, born in Alabama, wrote her first story at age nine and her first romance at thirteen. It wasn't until she spent three years working for the military behind the Iron Curtain—and a five-year stint with NASA—that she realized her true calling. Since then the *USA TODAY* bestselling author has penned more than one hundred novels, including her internationally bestselling Colby Agency series.

Regan Black, a *USA TODAY* bestselling author, writes award-winning, action-packed novels featuring kick-butt heroines and the sexy heroes who fall in love with them. Raised in the Midwest and California, she and her family, along with their adopted greyhound, two arrogant cats and a quirky finch, reside in the South Carolina Lowcountry, where the rich blend of legend, romance and history fuels her imagination.

Books by Debra Webb and Regan Black

Harlequin Intrigue

The Specialists: Heroes Next Door

The Hunk Next Door
Heart of a Hero
To Honor and To Protect
Her Undercover Defender

Visit the Author Profile page at
Harlequin.com for more titles.

CAST OF CHARACTERS

Terri Barnhart—A nurse at the MUSC Medical Center in Charleston, South Carolina, Terri has been juggling her career as well as caring for her brother, who barely survived the car crash that killed their parents.

David Martin—Raised on the Georgia coast, his scuba diving and underwater expertise have been useful to both the coast guard and Thomas Casey's team of elite Specialists.

Thomas Casey—The director of the Specialists must assemble one last task force to safeguard national interests before he can retire.

Trey Barnhart—Four years younger than Terri, he has struggled to overcome survivor's guilt and injuries sustained in the car crash that killed their parents and altered his college plans.

Dr. Franklin Palmer—A research scientist, he has developed a new biotechnology that could change the war on terror—if the terrorists don't steal it first.

Chapter One

David Martin had the training pool to himself. The fading sunlight filtered through the windows near the ceiling, casting long pale slashes across the deck. While other people finished paperwork or made dinner plans, he soaked up the peace and quiet of the water. It was his sanctuary, the one place he could always get away from any worries. The only thing better would be time out on the ocean—or under it. He hadn't had a real dive in months, and since his boat was stored closer to his family in Georgia, the pool would have to suffice for today.

He pushed his body through a freestyle sprint the length of the pool, filled his lungs on the turn and then dove deep, dolphin-kicking the return lap on that single breath. He repeated the process until the timer on his watch went off. Switching to backstroke, he let his body cool down. As his lungs recovered, his mind drifted over the implications of his upcoming meeting with his boss, Director Thomas Casey.

The brief email had bordered on cryptic, which wasn't unusual considering the unique covert operations team he'd joined two years ago. One specific phrase in the email had brought David down to swim and think: *lifetime assignment.*

He understood commitment as it pertained to career, family and country, having completed his education and given six years to the Coast Guard. Unfortunately, the phrase reminded him too much of the matchmaking his three oldest sisters kept attempting on his behalf. They used words like *stability, comfort, nieces* and *nephews.* As if their own kids didn't keep everyone busy enough. Curse of being the youngest and the only boy in a big Southern family, he thought. He loved them all and appreciated the buffer of distance his skills and career choices had given him. The Coast Guard had been a smart fit, and not even his sisters had ever worked up the nerve to argue about his professional dedication. Now, believing he worked a normal day job in DC, they manipulated blind dates and chance meetings every time he was home, hoping to reel him back in and settle him down near the family home.

They seemed impervious to his personal time-table. At thirty, he wasn't ready to do the wife and kids thing. He liked the excitement and the challenge of being a Specialist on Thomas Casey's elite team. While he understood that going out and making a difference in the world didn't rule out relationships—plenty of Specialists had personal lives—it sure put a damper on permanence. He wasn't ready for that. Not yet. There was plenty of time to find the right woman.

Lifetime assignment. The two words echoed through his head as his strokes sliced through the water. What kind of threat had Director Casey taking that kind of measure? He bounced around the pros and cons, despite the lack of specific information. It couldn't be anything anonymous like witness protection. Casey knew David maintained close ties to family, despite his near-obsessive meddling sisters. Whatever prompted this type of precaution, David knew he couldn't accept a permanent assignment in a landlocked area. Being raised on the Georgia coast, he needed the ocean as much as fresh air and sunshine.

His watch flashed and sounded another alarm, and David finished his lap. Pulling himself out of the pool, he sat at the edge, feet dangling in the water. It was silly to keep wondering. There was only one way to find out if Casey's lifetime assignment would suit him. Hearing the slap of flip-flops, he looked up and smiled. "Hey, Noah," he said, raising a hand. He and Noah Drake had discovered their mutual appreciation of the coast when they were tasked together on a water rescue mission. The fellow Specialist and artist maintained a house on one of Georgia's barrier islands and allowed David to use it when he wanted to dive in the area.

"Am I interrupting?" Noah inquired, tossing the towel in his hands onto a nearby chair.

"No. Just finished up and got lost in thought."

"It happens," Noah said with a commiserating smile. "I know this is early, but Blue is already planning the annual New Year's bash on the island. You're welcome to join us again."

"That could be good." Depending on his upcoming meeting. "I had a great time last year." It had been the ideal excuse to dodge the romantic trap his sisters had set in motion. "Thanks for the heads-up."

"Sure." Noah stepped back as David stood. "There's been some noise about a new shipwreck discovered nearby. I thought you'd like to take a look."

"Definitely." Any time he could get underwater was a good thing. His parents often joked he should have flippers and gills instead of feet and lungs. He rubbed a towel over his hair again and looped it around his neck. "Thanks, man."

"You got it," Noah said. "Just remember your friends if you find some unclaimed treasure."

David laughed to himself as Noah walked away. He rarely stopped to think about how much he appreciated the friends he'd made here. A lifetime assignment could mean the end of those connections. His mother's wisdom came to mind. Much as she'd done when he joined the Coast Guard, she'd remind him that moving on was part of life and that true friends and good family weren't limited by geography.

Pushing the questions to the back of his mind, he showered and dressed for the meeting. Director Casey didn't waste resources, human or otherwise, and David needed to go in prepared to listen and make a swift decision. Casey would expect nothing less.

David checked his reflection, satisfied with the pressed khakis and black cable-knit sweater. He pushed his thick, dark hair back from his face, missing the military regulation cut he'd maintained during his Coast Guard service. Specialists had to be less obvious and able to blend in with civilians, so he'd let it grow a bit longer since moving to Casey's team.

With an open mind and no small amount of curiosity, David rode the elevator to the offices upstairs. His shoes squeaked as he crossed the polished marble floor, and he grinned at the receptionist waiting for him when he swiped his key card and walked through the glass doors.

"Hey, Elizabeth. Is Director Casey ready for me?"

She nodded. "I'll let him know you're headed his way."

David gave a little double tap on the countertop surrounding her like a bunker. "Thanks."

With each step he coached himself to keep an open mind, to hear it all before he leaped in with both feet. Casey's door was open, but David knocked on the door anyway. His boss made eye contact over his computer monitor and waved him on in. David entered and closed the door behind him. He paused at the guest chairs, feeling an unexpected bout of nerves.

"Have a seat," Casey said. "You read the email?"

David nodded. "A few times."

"Good. I was just going over your employment and service records. Before we go any further, remember you can always turn down an assignment."

David had yet to meet a Specialist who'd done

that. "I'm hoping for more information before I make a commitment."

"Of course," Casey acknowledged.

He leaned back into what David termed a leadership pose, his hands resting lightly on the padded armrests of his executive chair. The body language appeared open, but David knew better. The director had forgotten more secrets than any of his Specialists had racked up.

"How do you feel about hospitals?" the boss asked.

David bit back the immediate questions, knowing Casey would provide information in good time. "As a lifetime assignment? I'm probably only qualified to be a janitor." He definitely didn't want to make a lasting career of mopping floors.

"We can do better than that," Casey promised. "If you agree to accept this post, you'll go in as yourself, with your service record intact through the Coast Guard years. We'll smooth over what you've done since."

So far so good, David thought. He could be himself, maintain the ties to friends and family and still be part of a bigger purpose.

"You'll be posted in Charleston, South Carolina, and we have plans to insert you as part of the staff at MUSC."

Having grown up in Georgia, David was

familiar with the shorthand reference for the Medical University of South Carolina facility. "My accent should fit right in there."

Casey exhibited a rare smile. "Agreed." He leaned forward, pushing a manila folder across the desk. "Aside from a decent-paying nine-to-five job, you could be a part of local dive communities and coastal action."

The director knew which buttons to push. "You sound like a recruiter promising me hobbies and a social life beyond the job," David said, wary of the inevitable catch. "I'm sure you didn't design this position for me."

Casey seemed to sigh without making a sound. "I want some long-range plans in place before I retire. Every day we hear more chatter about strikes aimed our way. Placing dedicated assets in key areas is the best way to safeguard our interests and prevent the loss of innocent lives.

"This is a lifetime placement. You'll still be a Specialist and expected to report as you would on any other mission," Casey went on. "If and when we encounter problems in Charleston or the general region, you'll be called to help."

Sounded too good to be true, and still David was interested. "Count me in."

"All right." Casey's nod showed more grit than approval or enthusiasm. "Charleston has a few choice targets from the ports to the nuclear school, to the prison at the Naval Weapons Station."

David's background and skills would be a more natural fit in any one of those places. He waited, stifling his rising curiosity, to hear the reason he was headed for a desk job inside the hospital instead.

"Intel has confirmed an immediate threat potential at MUSC. A research scientist has been working on implanted devices that could change the way we track criminals and people involved with terrorist actions. Despite precautions, word is out that he's nearly perfected the biotech. Naturally, as a matter of national security, we keep a close eye on things like this. The most recent reports indicate a terrorist cell *might*—I emphasize that for a reason—have a way to get close to him. We're working to clarify who knows what."

At the director's urging, David opened the manila folder and skimmed through the doctor's background. The official head shot for Dr. Franklin Palmer was accompanied by an extensive list of degrees, publications and apparent accomplishments.

"If you take this placement," Casey explained, "we'll get you inserted at the hospital and find a house for you near a nurse who works at MUSC.

The nurse has a close personal connection to Dr. Palmer."

David glanced up from the page outlining Palmer's early project. "These results are amazing."

"Yes," Casey agreed. "Unless the technology falls into the hands of our enemies."

"That's where I come in?"

"Primarily. You'll need to befriend the nurse, Terri Barnhart." He signaled for David to flip to a marker in the file. "We can't afford to let anyone use her as leverage against Palmer. Her brother went missing in early September, a month after he started college at Northern Arizona University. She reported him missing to local authorities when she became aware of the situation, but the investigation never really went anywhere."

David studied the candid picture of the nurse and her brother at what must have been move-in day. He noticed that Trey Barnhart at twenty-two was older than the average freshman. The stat made him curious. "For an adult, with no sign of foul play, why bother?"

"That would be why the investigation stalled out," Casey replied. "It seems the brother just gave up and walked away from school one day. Left all his personal belongings behind in his dorm room."

"Your sources say there's more to it?"

"Possibly," Casey allowed. "We don't have solid proof, but we think he's been picked up by a group called Rediscover near Sedona."

"Lots of New Age stuff out that way," David said.

Casey nodded. "This group can't seem to figure out if they're a peace-preaching cult or a terrorist cell. The public rhetoric centers on self-discovery, independence and less government. According to the few people who've parted ways with the group, the deeper you go in the process, the more you learn about the conspiracy theories and ugly intentions at the core. The financials are suspicious. A few questionable deals, some protests, along with a list of shady associates, has put them on the watch list."

"History of violence?"

"Yes. They are violent and very thorough. If Rediscover's leaders know about Dr. Palmer's research, they would've done their homework. Recruiting Trey Barnhart could give them the access or leverage they need to interfere with the project."

"Pretty convenient having someone connected to the doctor show up for school in Flagstaff."

"Exactly. My team has been playing catch-up on this, trying to pinpoint if the group targeted Trey from the beginning. It's all in the file."

David closed the folder and drummed his fingertips on it, weighing the options. "Sounds like I tell my family I've changed jobs. They'll be thrilled I'm relocating to Charleston. Close enough to visit on every holiday."

"Will that be a problem?"

"Not a bit." David shrugged. "I've had three decades of practice dealing with my sisters. I'm less sure about becoming a home owner." When Casey arched an eyebrow, he quickly added, "Just kidding. If you want me in Charleston, that's where I'll be. Any rules on communications?"

"The typical mission parameters will be in place," Casey explained. "You can always call in if there's a problem. We'll provide new intel as it comes in. You'll be on the front lines, but the Specialists will always have your back."

"And after you retire?"

"You won't be forgotten. My replacement will be fully briefed on your ongoing mission."

"Guess I'd better pack and tell my landlord I'm out."

"Take another minute," Casey cautioned. "This is a serious, permanent commitment that will last far beyond Dr. Palmer's project. I won't think any less of you if you turn it down."

David wanted to accept the post immediately. Instead, he took the director's advice and stood and crossed the well-appointed office to the window. He shoved his hands into his pockets and just soaked up the view. Several stories below, beyond a heavy tree line, the cityscape sparkled on the horizon. "I won't be mopping floors?" he asked without turning.

Casey chuckled. "No. We're working you into the human resources department."

David absorbed that detail, though he'd made his decision when the director mentioned Charleston. He hadn't been there in years, but he had fond memories. His biggest concern was whether or not he could handle the routine of a nine-to-five job. He'd started working at the age of eleven mowing yards and washing cars. When he'd learned to scuba dive he'd worked his way through high school and college leading dive tours and helping with rescues. The closest he'd come to a normal job had been his time with the Coast Guard. There had been daily routines and drills, but the work had never been static or boring.

It was Charleston, he thought, shifting his focus. The day job wasn't the point; it was the cover. Between the real mission and the area in general, if the day job dragged there would always be something to keep him busy after hours. He turned around, walked back to Casey's desk and eyed the closed folder. "I'm in."

Casey stood and reached across the desk to shake David's hand. "Thank you for your service," he said, his tone grave.

The director's demeanor was a bit unnerving. Thomas Casey always maintained a serious calm during a briefing. Either the job or this particular assignment rested heavier than most across his shoulders.

"Head down to the equipment room and they'll get you set for an immediate transition."

David said goodbye and walked out, wondering when he'd see the director or the team offices again. He didn't know much about human resources, though he could learn. Getting up to speed on a desk job would be much faster than posing as a medical tech or expert. His boss wanted him in Charleston sooner rather than later to protect the project. Looking at the surface details on this doctor, the nurse and the missing brother, David knew some sort of serious adventure was guaranteed.

And that was just the type of work he thrived on.

Chapter Two

Charleston, South Carolina
Tuesday, December 10, 6:55 a.m.

At the nurses station in the center of the pediatric orthopedic ward, Terri Barnhart reviewed patient charts as she prepared to take over the day shift. She'd been moved up here last month, and most days they had more trouble with anxious parents than the patients themselves.

"Room 412 needs a warning label," her friend Suzette said quietly, looking over her shoulder. "The girl cried when MaryAnn took her vitals."

Terri quickly scrolled through the patient's record. Ten years old, the girl was recovering from her second surgery on a broken leg. "Wow," Terri whispered. "She's afraid of everything, isn't she?"

Suzette nodded. "Just about the worst case of hospital phobia I've seen. Her mom's a dream, but exhausted. We tried everything last night.

Maybe you'll get lucky and she'll sleep through your shift."

Terri shared a quiet laugh with Suzette. "I'll let you know if I figure her out." She was known around the hospital for her ability to cope with more difficult patients. She considered it a by-product of helping her brother recover from the car accident that killed their parents, grateful something good had come out of that tragedy.

Thinking of Trey sobered her. She hadn't heard from him for three months now. What had been an all-consuming worry when she found out he'd dropped out of college became tangled with a little more anger every day. The police were certain he'd just gone off on his own, but if that was true, why hadn't he contacted her?

They'd been close as kids, through school and sports, right up to the day of her pinning ceremony when she graduated from the nursing program four years ago. Trey and their parents had been on their way to the auditorium eager to celebrate her success. A dump truck swerved into their lane and hit them head-on. Her parents died at the scene, and her brother had been plunged into the fight of his life.

His extensive injuries had ended his plans to play college baseball. Several surgeries, months of physical therapy and hours of grief counseling had finally put him back together. Or so she'd thought as he eventually changed his career goals and applied to college.

She couldn't reconcile Trey's effort and determination to attend school in Arizona with him willingly leaving it all behind scarcely a month after arriving there. If the police in Flagstaff sympathized with her, it didn't motivate them to make his disappearance a priority.

Thanksgiving had come and gone without a word from her brother, and Christmas was closing in. If he was alive and well—and she had to believe that—he would make contact. He had to know she would be worried about him, that she'd need some reassurance especially during the holidays. She trembled as another terrible image of him injured or worse filled her mind.

"Honey, are you okay?" Suzette asked, waving her hand in front of Terri's face.

"I'm great." Terri pasted a bright smile on her face. "Just waiting for the second cup of coffee to kick in."

"Right." Suzette stretched out the single word. "Still no word from him?"

As her best friend, Suzette was one of the few people who knew the whole situation about Trey. Suzette had helped her sort out the insurance, funeral arrangements and expenses after the accident. She'd listened to the doctors' reports and helped her make the decisions Trey would have to live with. Suzette had sat by Trey's bedside, taking over when Terri had been too sleep deprived to continue.

"No," Terri admitted. "You'll be happy to know I'm counting by the week now rather than the day or hour."

"I suppose that's progress," Suzette said. "If you need to vent, you know I'll listen."

Terri took a deep breath and looped her stethoscope around her neck. "I'm grateful, believe me, but I can't tell you how nice it is to have other people to think about for the next eight to ten hours."

Suzette's smile turned edgy. "Promise me one thing."

"What's that?"

"When he comes home—and I believe he will—I get first crack at whipping his butt."

A smile, the first genuine one in a while, tugged at the corners of Terri's mouth. "Right after me."

"Just as long as I get to watch," Suzette declared.

As Suzette started for the elevator, Terri promised to call her later and then headed for room 412. Her first order of business on every shift was to introduce herself to her patients. In orthopedics, the majority of their patients were simply here for observation after surgery. The post-op process was more about managing pain and mobility than anything else. And fear, she thought, easing open the door of 412, temporary home to the young and frightened Brittney Markwald. The girl's mother had pulled a chair close to the bed and was reading from a thick book.

Terri smiled, recognizing the popular story, but as soon as Brittney saw her, she stared to cry. Terri stopped and tucked her hands into her pockets. "Good morning. I'm Terri, your nurse for today." She focused on the mother. "Mrs. Markwald, I've reviewed the chart and everything looks great. The doctor should be in to see you before noon."

"Will he send us home?"

"I can't give you a definite answer on that, but as soon as I know something, you will, too." She looked at Brittney but didn't come any closer to the bed. "How're you doing with the crutches today?"

"She's getting better," Mrs. Markwald replied when Brittney only sniffled. "We just got back from the bathroom."

"Great," Terri said to the mother. "Your doctor will be happy to hear that." She took care of the things that needed her attention, giving Brittney plenty of space.

"How's the pain level?" Terri asked from the foot of the bed.

The girl's lower lip quivered as she shrugged.

Terri had to find a way to crack through the child's fear. "Can I check the ice in your friend there?" She pointed to the small cooler that circulated ice water through a cuff to keep swelling to a minimum.

The girl shook her head, refusing to make eye contact. Suzette might be onto something with this one.

"I just refilled it," Mrs. Markwald explained with a weary smile. "My husband had one a few months back after a knee surgery."

"So you're a pro." Terri beamed. "Thanks so much. Be sure to press the button if you need me. I'll pop in later to take your vitals."

Sniffles from the bed accompanied the mother's thank-you as Terri left the room. Phobic patients like Brittney weren't unusual on this floor, but Terri never stopped trying to make a hospital stay as pleasant as possible for everyone. Stress didn't help the healing process.

After introducing herself to her other patients, she caught one of the nursing techs on the floor for help moving a few things around in the lounge. It was a long shot, but she'd made it her mission for the shift to get at least one smile out of Brittney before her doctor sent her home. If nothing else, it might make life easier for a nurse in Brittney's future.

Terri returned to 412, this time waiting until Mrs. Markwald reached a stopping point in the story. "Breakfast is coming around," she explained. "You can have it in here or you can really impress the doctors."

After a moment of visible skepticism, Brittney asked, "How?"

Contact at last, Terri thought with an inner cheer. "You're doing well enough that you can eat down in the lounge. There's a video game kart racing challenge and we post high scores on the wall."

"You mean I don't have to stay in here?"

Terri nodded. "You can stay in the room if you like. But if you want to go to the lounge, I can have physical therapy meet you there, too."

Brittney's momentary excitement faded. "I don't want more people messing with me."

"Well, that's understandable, but you don't get to go home until they know you can manage the crutches."

Brittney aimed another sullen expression at her mother.

"It's a lot more fun, I promise," Terri added. "Unless you're tired."

"I'm not tired," Brittney declared. "I want to go."

Brittney cooperated as Terri and her mother helped her get settled in front of one of the lounge gaming stations. When she was engrossed with outfitting her racer, Terri pulled the mother aside. "You can go down to the cafeteria for breakfast and coffee," she suggested. "I double-checked with the surgeon's office. He won't be up for another hour at least."

"What if—"

"Your daughter will be fine with us. If the surgeon's schedule changes, I'll call you."

The mother's eyes brightened with relief. "Thank you," she said, slipping out of her daughter's sight. "She's not usually such a handful. They did their best last night, but…"

"She's upset and scared. Happens to all of us at some point." Terri had been blessed with good health, but she understood the fears and questions that plagued her patients. "We'll get you through this as a team."

With Brittney happily distracted, Terri moved on through her shift, tending to patient calls and overseeing discharge orders. The hours sped by and her rumbling stomach cued her in that she needed to eat and she headed downstairs to the cafeteria. Normally, she brought lunch from home, but after another restless night full of anxious dreams about her brother she'd overslept. In the subsequent rush to get out the door, she'd left her lunch bag sitting on the kitchen counter.

Reminders from the police and her friends

that Trey was officially a legal adult and smart enough to get into college failed to ease her worry over his disappearance. After the first month with no word from him, she'd sought the help of the best private investigator she could afford. Unfortunately, her modest investment only confirmed what his college roommate had told her. Trey had changed almost overnight, going from an outgoing freshman making friends on campus to withdrawn and reclusive until he went out one day and just didn't return.

Letting him go to college in Arizona had been a mistake, Terri knew that now. It had been too big a leap. His body had been ready, thanks to his hard work through physical therapy, but she never should've accepted his claim about his emotional stability at face value. If nothing else, her constant worry was proof she hadn't been ready to be this far from him.

She loved her friends and her work, but she was lonely without her brother. He was the only family she had left. On move-in day, she'd taken plenty of pictures and, before she left, they'd tossed around ideas for the holiday break between semesters. Now Christmas was only two weeks away, and she didn't know what she was supposed to do without him.

"Hey, Terri."

Startled, she glanced up at the sound of her

name and then smiled into the rugged, handsome face of David Martin. "Oh. Hey, David."

He was relatively new at the hospital and he'd made an impression on most of the women with his Georgia accent, that dark hair and those eyes that were more gray than blue. Somehow on him, the pressed khakis, white polo shirt and dark blue fleece jacket embroidered with the MUSC logo looked as though it belonged on the cover of *GQ*.

She suddenly felt a little silly in her bright, tropical frog scrubs. "How's your day going?"

"Predictable." He lifted his tall coffee mug. "I came looking for a shot of caffeine. Reports are due in a couple of hours." He checked his watch. "Late lunch?" He dipped his chin in the direction of the plastic salad container she held.

"Yeah. The lunch I packed is still sitting at home."

"Want some company?"

That would be lovely. She always enjoyed talking with him over coffee or lunch. "I wish I could take a few minutes down here," she said. "There's a problem child on the ward today and I don't want to give her any reason to get upset again."

He grinned, and the tilt of his lips set butterflies loose in her belly. "You applied that famous Nurse Terri charm, didn't you?"

She laughed. "Of course." She leaned a little closer, just because she could. "It's possible this patient's immune."

"I don't believe that for a minute." He nudged her shoulder. "No one's immune to that smile."

Her lips curved even more at the words, and his confidence gave her mood a much-needed boost. "Thanks."

"We're still on for tonight, right?"

She nodded. He'd invited her to dinner at a new place on King Street. If she didn't get back upstairs, she wouldn't have any time at all to eat. She tried to care, but food seemed far less important than taking a few minutes with an interesting man like David. "I'll be ready."

"Great." He followed her into the elevator and punched the button for her floor.

"What are you doing?" Whenever they did get together over lunch, they parted ways at the elevator.

His dark eyebrows arched. "Walking you back," he said. "Is that a problem?"

"No." It was just different. She remembered how the gossip had zipped through the hospital when he joined the staff in October. Handsome as sin was the first gossip that made the circuit. He was athletic and absolutely ripped, according to those who'd spent time in the fitness center with him. But his humor, his humility and the manners proving chivalry wasn't dead had made him an instant hit among the women.

So she'd heard of him long before he introduced himself during his second week of work. He'd been in line behind her during a coffee break and they'd hit it off when he'd asked about the best beaches for sea kayaking. In the weeks since, they'd had lunch occasionally and frequently chatted over coffee. They'd even gone on a sea kayak excursion, as well as a couple of evening art showcases at the Market. She'd been careful to keep the social speculation to a minimum and she'd been relieved to hear he was making friends quickly in several departments.

It wasn't that she didn't want a social life—she did. She'd just been too consumed with Trey's disappearance to be good company. Something about sharing coffee or lunch with David was less intimidating than going out on a date or out for drinks with friends. With David, she didn't feel the pressure to be on. She could just relax and be herself. Of his many positive traits, that one was her favorite, though she couldn't tell anyone. Not even Suzette. Her friends would read way too much into any positive comments she made about David or any other guy.

Her friends had been setting her up since Trey moved to college in August. The few guys she'd met had been nice, but she'd needed time and space to recharge her personal batteries after spending years dealing with Trey's physical injuries and challenging fits of temper. Not that she blamed him for acting out as he came to terms with the fact that his dreams and goals were out of reach. As he'd told her repeatedly, he'd suffered the most. They'd both lost their parents, but Terri had her dream job and Trey never would.

Now he was missing and she felt caught in another emotional quagmire, keeping to herself simply so she wouldn't dump her drama on others. She thought of young Brittney, afraid of practically every element of life since she'd broken her leg. Like a lightning strike, Terri suddenly realized, wallowing in worry wasn't doing her any more good than it was Brittney. Being available 24/7, afraid to miss a call or text from her brother was a waste of her time. She had to break out of this holding pattern.

"Hey," David said. "You okay in there?"

"Sorry." She felt the heat climbing into her cheeks. The elevator chimed at her floor. "Just distracted..." The doors parted, and she stepped out, pausing in the doorway for a second. She needed to voice her new resolve. "I won't be distracted tonight. I'm looking forward to it."

David's mouth tipped up at one corner. "Me, too."

She held his gaze until the doors closed between them, feeling her mouth curve in an answering grin. She turned toward the staff area, her salad suddenly looking more appetizing. Tonight was as good a time as any to move forward with her life, and who better to take that step with than a nice new guy-friend like David?

No matter what her friends would say, he hadn't invited her out on an actual real date. They were just friends. Right now it was enough to think of herself first for a change. David was attractive, thoughtful and fun. Tonight would be great, no specific definition required.

Chapter Three

David set the laminated menu down and waited for Terri's reaction. He'd chosen a small, quirky restaurant on King Street for dinner. He wasn't quite sure how to play it—as a date or another outing with a friend. Typically they saw each other at work when her hair was pulled back and she wore shapeless scrubs and he was in the requisite logo-crested apparel. Tonight, she looked beautiful in dark jeans that hugged her fit body and a sage sweater that made her green eyes pop. She'd left her caramel-brown hair down, and the lights pulled out all those golden tones in the glossy, shoulder-length waves.

However she might be defining tonight, this place kept the mood light and easy for both of them. With nearly two dozen variations on classic mac and cheese, he'd wanted to give it a try for some time. Based on her smile and eager expression, he'd made the right call. "What do you think?"

"It's like comfort food with a gourmet twist." When she met his gaze, her eyes were dancing with mischief. "Anything I order will render my workout absolutely useless and I can't wait. It all sounds delicious."

"Good." The dining area was small and casual, but David had felt weird about eating here alone. It was a quirky by-product of being the youngest of four kids. He'd been raised with loud, boisterous conversation around a dinner table loaded with food every night. Although he enjoyed quiet meals alone at home, eating out was somehow different. "Have you heard the Battery Lane band before?"

"Yes!" she said as her soft green eyes lit up. "Suzette and I caught them when they played one of the beach bars on Isle of Palms this summer."

"They're down at Benny's tonight. I thought we could swing by for a bit after we eat."

"Sounds great," she agreed. "Be warned I turn into a pumpkin around midnight this week."

"No problem. Shift work can be a bear. I did plenty of that in the Coast Guard."

The waitress came by, and they placed their orders, each of them choosing a different gourmet combination.

"I took every shift I could get my hands on

just out of nursing school," she said when the waitress walked away. "Usually I adapt quickly. Or maybe my body's resigned to getting fewer hours of sleep."

He liked that she could laugh at herself. "Must have been hard times starting your career in the midst of losing your parents."

"It wasn't easy," she admitted. "Trey's injuries and the survivor guilt issues complicated things." Her smile was a little sad. "But he's *fine*," she said, putting air quotes around the word. "Somehow we made it."

David didn't want to prod a sore spot, but with the holidays coming up, everyone concerned was hoping Trey would make contact with his sister. Human intel in Arizona had dried up and they really needed to figure out if Rediscover intended to make good on veiled threats against Dr. Palmer's work. "That's what counts. These past years couldn't have been easy. I'm not sure how I'll cope when we lose our parents."

"I hope it's a long ways off for you," she said, her eyes going misty. "I miss them every day." She traced the rim of her water glass with her fingertip. "Can we talk about something else? This close to the holidays…" Her voice trailed off and she wrinkled her nose.

"Sure." His task of keeping an eye on Terri was progressing smoothly. He enjoyed her company, but Casey had alerted him this morning that Dr. Palmer would be moving a trial patient into MUSC for the final adjustments and testing. It would be a prime opportunity for Rediscover to strike. "Do you have your Christmas tree up yet?"

"No. You?"

He shook his head. "I'm trying to decide if I'll go artificial or real or skip it altogether this year." He shrugged. "I'll be going to Georgia, so the tree would be just for me, y'know?"

"Don't skip it," she said. "Which were you raised with?"

"Artificial. My mom squeezes out every minute of the holiday season. She puts the tree up bright and early the Friday after Thanksgiving. The high could be eighty and she'll have Christmas carols cranked up and a vat of hot cocoa going all day." He leaned forward. "I nearly resigned when my department gave us all a four-day weekend. I had no excuses. Everyone who's home for more than Thanksgiving Day gets sucked into her decorating vortex."

As he'd hoped, Terri laughed along with him. "You love it," she accused.

"I love my mom," he agreed. "I'll admit the holiday chaos is more fun now that there's a few nieces and nephews underfoot."

"I bet." Her gaze drifted away and her smile faded.

"Hey." He waved his hand in front of her face. "Did I bum you out?"

"Not at all. I was just imagining how it must be for you."

She tried to cover it, but her stiff, stubborn smile was proof the conversation was a downer. The expression was too similar to the one she wore in the photo on her employee badge. The picture had been taken just ten days after her parents died. Though he wanted to know about her traditions and holiday plans, he didn't want to ruin the entire evening just because he had a job to do. Information collecting was, unfortunately, necessary.

"When will Trey be home for the holidays?"

"Well." She tilted her head side to side and took too much interest in the placement of her fork. "I'm not exactly sure."

"He *is* coming home?"

She cleared her throat and reached for her water, her gaze roaming over the eclectic decor. "He tells me he really likes Arizona and he's making friends. I think the distance is good for him this year. Maybe for me, too."

She still didn't trust him enough to share her concerns about her missing brother. "You should be together," David said.

"We've been almost inseparable thanks to our circumstances. It's possible he's trying to help by staying out there."

"How so?"

"By not expecting me to come up with airfare."

"That makes sense, I guess." Except money wasn't the real issue. David wanted to find Trey and jerk him up by his ears and tell him to treat his sister with more respect. Too bad he couldn't reveal his protective streak as her newest friend. Even without the background and intel, he'd heard plenty about Terri's rough time with Trey. The stories of her devotion to his recovery and her never-quit work ethic were common knowledge around the hospital.

David made a decision on the spot. Assuming his assignment didn't change, he promised himself that whether or not Trey posed a threat to Dr. Palmer's research project, he wouldn't let him take advantage of Terri or continue to run roughshod over her feelings. After everything she'd been through, everything she'd overcome, she deserved better.

Like a spy pretending to be her pal? The annoying little voice in his head had been nagging him almost since the beginning. The trouble was, he liked Terri more with every passing conversation. She was a kind person and a damn fine nurse. If anyone needed a break from trouble, it was her. Too bad her brother wasn't on the same page.

David told himself he and Trey were nothing alike. Neither of them was being completely honest with her, but David wasn't running around with a bunch of extremists who spouted peace and delivered violence.

"It sounds like you have a great family," Terri said as their salads were delivered.

"Believe me, there were plenty of days I wished I was an only child," he said with a wink. He'd told her about his older sisters and the blind date fiasco they'd arranged during his Thanksgiving visit.

She'd laughed long and hard at that one. "You know your sisters mean well."

He rolled his eyes and groaned. "The matchmaking meddlers need to find a different hobby. Maybe you could give them a course in minding their own business. You never talk about setting up blind dates for your brother."

Oops. He noticed immediately he'd taken the wrong tack. He gave himself a mental kick as her eyes clouded with worry. She poked at her salad for a few minutes and changed the subject. He didn't know if he should apologize or just let it go.

She pushed her half-eaten salad aside with a sigh. "The truth is I may never have that chance."

"What do you mean?"

"My brother dropped out of college." She bit her lip before continuing. "He hasn't contacted me at all in months. I don't have any idea where he is or if he ever plans to come home."

David didn't have to fake the surprise. He couldn't believe she was telling him this. Despite what it meant for the case, he hated that she suffered over it. "Terri, I'm sorry."

She swallowed. "Me, too. I won't bore you with all the gory details and I don't want to dwell on it tonight. I just thought you should know in case... I don't know." She sucked in a breath. "In case I seem sad over the next couple of weeks."

He nodded, wishing he felt as though she'd welcome his touch. She looked like a woman who could use a hug. They'd shared coffee breaks, lunches and various activities around town, but they'd kept it completely platonic. "Come spend Christmas with us."

"Pardon?"

Good Lord, had he really just said that? Casey wanted him to get close to her, not adopt her. "I'm serious." He had to be. It was too late to back down. "We're crazy, sure, but we're fun. You'll have a blast."

"Your sisters will really ramp up the match-making attempts if you bring a woman home."

"Let's burn that bridge when we get there." He wasn't about to let this go, but he waited while the waitress delivered Terri's choice of steak and bleu cheese and his bowl of lobster mac and cheese in front of him.

"Oh, wow." She picked up her fork and assembled a bite of cheesy pasta and sliced beef. "This smells delicious."

"I second that." He scooped up lobster mac and cheese from his wide bowl. "This is amazing. How's yours?"

"Fabulous," she said. "Try a bite." She nudged her bowl his way.

He indulged her before returning to the previous topic. "What would you tell a patient facing the holidays alone?"

She shook her head. "I've never worked the psych ward."

"No, but you've worked every other ward."

"Almost."

"Just answer the question."

"Eat your dinner," she countered, leading by example and closing her lips around a bite of her cheesy pasta. She pointed to his plate when he hesitated. "Eat."

He did as she said, and all thought of conversation halted while they enjoyed the excellent food. "This has ruined me for normal mac and cheese," he said after a few minutes.

"Definitely." She ate a few more bites of her food, then leaned back and blotted her lips with the napkin. "I'd tell a patient to go be with friends," she said abruptly. "That doesn't mean I'll go to Georgia with you. It's not the same thing. But I do appreciate the invitation."

"It's exactly the same thing."

She rolled her eyes. "What if your sisters think I'm more than your friend?"

He exaggerated a contemplative expression. "That could have some happy side effects. Think of all the blind dates I wouldn't have to endure."

She laughed. "I'm thinking of all the heart-broken women who were looking forward to an evening out with you."

"Well, you can write up a report of our evening and my sisters can distribute it. Those heart-broken women can live vicariously." He signaled for the check. "We have a band to catch."

She reached for her purse to help with the check, but he took care of it. "Chivalry may be dead in some places, but my mama would kill me if I let you pay."

She held up her hands, surrendering. "I don't want to be the cause of your demise," she said, chuckling.

After he'd paid the bill, they headed down the

street toward the bar. One of his favorite things about this part of the country was the reliable weather. They had a clear night, with a moon just past full hanging in the sky and an interesting woman at his side. Life was good.

"Thanks for a fantastic dinner," she said as they walked down King Street toward the bar.

"My pleasure. I'm glad you came with me. It bugs me to eat alone in public," he confessed.

She glanced up at him. "You must do a lot of cooking, then."

"I've learned a few skills. A guy's gotta eat."

"A girl, too," she said with a grin. "Cooking for one can get old in a hurry, though."

They joined the line of music fans waiting to enter Benny's. "Is that a subtle way of inviting me to dinner at your place?"

Her smile stretched wide. "Maybe."

"Thought so. I eat anything and everything except Brussels sprouts."

"Even if I roast them in coconut oil?"

"Veggies scented with suntan lotion." He winced. "That doesn't sound like a good plan."

"Then I'll come up with something better, I promise."

"Thanks," he said as they entered the bar and joined the fans eager for Battery Lane to get started. He caught her watching him and asked about it.

"Sorry. I pegged you for more Beach Boys and less Garth Brooks."

"You think you're the only one allowed to have eclectic tastes? I like a lot of things," he teased as he smiled into her pretty face.

The comment brought a warm blush to her cheeks, or maybe that was just the crowd packed tightly all around them. Regardless, it looked good on her. The band took the stage to an enthusiastic roar from the crowd. David was able to relax and enjoy the music and the woman beside him.

Knowing she had an early shift, he kept an eye on the time. He paid their tab and led her outside after the second set. "Want to take a walk down by the water?"

"I'd like that," she said, turning with him toward the Battery. "It's a nice evening."

They strolled past historic mansions glowing with holiday lights until they reached the park at the peninsula. The sound of the water and the gentle breeze coming in off the harbor put a nice cap on what amounted to a perfect evening.

"Did you have fun?"

"I must not have shown it well if you have to ask." She paused, leaning back against the rail and gazing up into the sky. "I've had the best time, David. Thank you. Next time, dinner is on me."

"That depends," he hedged.

"On what?"

"On whether the next time we go out it's a date."

"Oh."

He waited for more of a reaction, but she walked on in silence, her face turned away from him, looking at something out in the harbor.

"Did I make you uncomfortable?"

"No. It's just me," she said quietly. "Between work and Trey, I haven't taken much time to socialize."

"You and I have socialized quite a bit," he pointed out.

"As friends," she said. "I've enjoyed it."

"Fair enough." He let it go, for now. "We don't have to decide anything tonight."

Her footsteps slowed, and she pulled her jacket tight across her body. He suddenly wanted to wrap her in his arms and shelter her from the cool breeze and anything else taking aim at her. He shook off the feeling. Friendship was one thing. If he started believing the role he was playing, he was doomed to fail the mission and the woman.

Except this wasn't just a role, this was his new life. "It should be a date," he blurted. They stopped again and he studied her face in the moonlight, wishing for some insight.

"It can't be," she said.

The depth of his disappointment surprised him. "Why not?"

"Because if this *was* a date, I'd be nervous and that would ruin it. It's been ages since I was on a date. Out with a friend is better."

"All right." They walked on in silence as he contemplated her logic. "Would you agree that we're two unattached people taking a stroll that might be interpreted as romantic?"

"By whom?" She glanced around, and the wind caught her hair. She shook it back from her face. "Stop teasing. Let's just enjoy the moment."

"I don't know if I can." He liked teasing her, liked the sparkle it put in her soft green eyes. "Not having a precise definition for tonight might ruin the evening for *me*."

She laughed, giving him a light elbow jab to his side. "That ballad in the last set warped your brain."

He denied the accusation and changed the subject. "Would you like to go out with me on the boat sometime?"

"As friends?"

That definition was better than pushing for something more that appeared to be destined to backfire. Having spent so much time avoiding serious relationships, he'd never had a girlfriend on his boat. Only guys and family had joined him for fishing or diving. "Friends bring the bait," he warned as they turned back toward the garage on King Street where he'd parked his car. "That's my rule."

"You just made that up."

He draped an arm over her shoulders. "You'll never prove it." They both chuckled. "Do you like to fish?"

"I'm not sure I remember how. It's been a long time."

"Not for me. I'll give you a refresher course."

"I'd like that."

"I guarantee you'll have a great time."

TERRI BELIEVED HIM. Somewhere in the past few weeks David had become the balance her life needed. She couldn't be all about the work, and she'd vowed to stop worrying over her brother. Or at least she'd vowed to worry less about him.

David's arm around her shoulders felt nice. Like his friendship, his arm was solid and steady and warm without the weight of pressure or expectations. On the way to the parking garage, they chatted more about fishing and his love of underwater diving. She loved to listen to him. His passion was contagious and he made her want to take a class and get certified. It would be a good, healthy hobby and something completely new.

She needed new and healthy things to start closing the gaps of her fractured family. It was frustrating to think about her first Christmas alone in the house where she'd grown up. She needed someone to share all those memories of her family traditions with. Maybe she should take David up on his outrageous offer and immerse herself in the happy chaos with his family. He didn't say things he didn't mean, she knew that, and his family sounded like good, fun people. Trying something new, if only for a day or two, would be healthier than her original plan of taking on extra shifts over the holiday week.

"Is it work?" he asked as he merged with the light traffic on the interstate. "Something has you distracted."

"Kind of." She paused for courage, holding her chilled hands in front of the heating vent. "I'd planned to work extra shifts, but if you were serious about the Christmas invitation, I'd like to accept it."

"Fantastic," he replied, sounding as sincere now as he had when he'd extended the invite. "My mom will be thrilled."

"You're sure it won't throw everyone into a tizzy?"

"In my house the philosophy is always the

more the merrier. I'll be sure they understand we're not…you know."

"Not what?" she asked, wanting to tease him a little. The way he said it, she had one of those rare and forbidden images of something physical with David. He might be handsome and sexy, but that didn't make it any more appropriate to imagine jumping her new friend. The last thing she wanted to do was to botch a friendship that was working so well. This wasn't the right time for serious or involved. Maybe it was finally her time—her time to discover what she wanted beyond work and responsibilities.

"Dating."

Oh, how she wished he'd never brought up the dating question. None of these thoughts would be plaguing her if the conversation hadn't come up. When he pulled into her driveway a few minutes later, she hurried to find her house key. She turned to thank him for a fun night, only to see he was coming around to open her car door.

Like a date.

"I can be a gentleman even if this isn't a date," he reminded her.

She thanked him and climbed out. He walked her all the way to the door. On the porch, key in hand, she suddenly didn't want to unlock the door. The moment she did that, this wonderful evening impersonating a normal woman *not* on a date would be over.

"If this was a date," she began, not quite able to look him in the eye, "I'd be getting butterflies right now."

"Butterflies?" He tucked his hands in his pockets. "Over me?"

"You know, about the…kiss." She did not just say that. Humiliation crowded into her throat.

"Ah…the kiss."

She looked up and the grin on his face, as much as the twinkle of mischief in his eyes, made her relax. Thank goodness, he wasn't reading too much into her silly confession. She'd let herself get carried away. They were friends. Friends who shared a taste for loud music, cheese-covered pasta, the ocean and excellent craft beer. The truth was she needed a friend more than a lover.

"Thanks for a great night, David."

"I'm glad we did this," he said. "It was almost perfect."

A frown tugged at her brow. "Almost?"

His gray eyes were dark as his gaze dropped to her mouth. He leaned in and his warm hands rested lightly on her shoulders. Her breath caught and she knew with a sudden and lovely clarity that this night truly was moving into date territory. The butterflies that had been swirling in her belly moments before quieted as his lips met hers.

The kiss, sweet and gentle, was full of promise and over too soon. The brisk night air rushed between them, cooling her lips, but it couldn't erase the underlying heat that set her body tingling.

"Good night, Terri." He stepped back.

"Good night, David."

She slipped inside and leaned back against the door, content to wait there until her knees stopped quaking. She licked her lips, catching the subtle taste of him there.

"Oh, my," she whispered when she heard his car leaving the driveway. Moving forward with her life, putting herself first, had some definite perks.

Suddenly, she couldn't recall why on earth she'd been so reluctant to make that move.

Chapter Four

David drove the few blocks to his own place on an unexpected high and far less conflicted than he should've been about that kiss. He enjoyed being with Terri and after that quick taste of her, he felt himself wanting more. He pulled into his garage rationalizing his actions with the reminder that it was important to be normal during an undercover op.

Except this wasn't a short-term, bust-the-bad-guy-and-get-out kind of thing. He flipped on the kitchen light and looked around, still a bit startled he had an entire house to himself. Three bedrooms, two-and-a-half baths, with a recently remodeled kitchen—it was a lot for one person. He'd had his share of roomy apartments, but a house was different.

Maybe it was his upbringing. A house was a tangible sign of commitment and meant for family. He wasn't ready for the family part of that equation, though he'd happily signed on for the home owner commitment and permanence. The location was ideal. Close enough to everything he loved about the water and far enough from his parents and sisters for privacy.

The real job, under the cover, promised everything he needed to stay challenged and active in the work he relished. In his few weeks here, he'd been exploring the area and history during his free time so he could be prepared to address a variety of threats. Although Trey Barnhart and his associates were the current problem, David would still be here long after any attacks on Dr. Palmer's research. He had to build a life and he didn't want that life to be a complete lie.

As Terri's friend, he didn't want his cover to hurt her and yet he couldn't risk telling her the truth. He liked her and he'd asked how to define the evening because he needed to know which approach to take as they moved forward. It was completely possible her brother would never return. David felt a little stab of guilt for thinking it because he could picture the sadness in her eyes if she never heard from her brother again.

"What a mess." He hooked his key ring on the wooden banana tree. The housewarming gift, intended for the kitchen counter and hanging bananas, had come from his oldest sister. She had touted the importance of proper fruit care as a current homeowner and future husband. He, in turn, had sent her a picture along with a text message thanking her for the cool key hook. So far, she hadn't bothered him with more lectures on responsibility. He didn't expect the reprieve to last.

At the kitchen table, he emptied his pockets and draped his coat over the back of a chair. Terri had mentioned her ability to run on only a few hours of sleep and he was much the same. Good thing, too. He was amped after that kiss. It would've been so easy to pull her into his arms and linger over it. To hold her close as he discovered how she liked to be kissed and what made her heart race. He wasn't sure which one of them would be more spooked by that move.

At least now he knew she was open to the idea of being more than friends, which would make it easier to stay close and involved if her brother made contact or showed up again.

He poured himself a tall glass of water, picked up his phone and headed into the den to check his email, along with the headlines and police reports on his laptop. He left no stone unturned in his perpetual search for Trey Barnhart. His phone rang and he waited for the caller ID display before answering.

He recognized the number. "Hello, Director Casey." The greeting would let his boss know he was alone.

"Have you checked your email?"

"Just doing that now."

"Good," Casey said. "We got a hit on Barnhart's passport at BWI earlier this afternoon."

"Returning from where?" Arriving at Baltimore Washington International Airport, he could be coming from most anywhere.

"Germany. We're assessing how long he stayed and where he went, but it's slow."

David refused to jump to any conclusions without more information. Trey visiting Germany could mean a variety of things from cars to biomedical research to being a groupie for one of the alternative rock bands always cropping up over there.

"He didn't rent a car at BWI," Casey added. "Or do anything else with a credit card. I can't be sure of his whereabouts since he landed."

"I understand." This elevated his alert status.

"Our profiler thinks he'll head your way, if only to see his sister."

"Holiday nostalgia," David said in full agreement, recalling what Terri had told him about her brother.

"That's a best-case scenario."

"Got it." David changed screens and brought up the feed on the bugs he'd planted in Terri's house. Reluctant to violate her privacy, he rarely listened in, but he would have to now.

"Are there docs over there working on the same tech as Palmer?"

"Possible, but the consensus is that no one is as close to this breakthrough as Dr. Palmer. That doesn't rule out a buyer intent on reverse engineering his device. I'm told the doctor is bringing that trial patient into the secure ward at the hospital any day now. It's possible Barnhart has undergone training to know what to ask and what to look for."

The news gave David a chill as he considered how Trey might use his sister to get inside the hospital computer system. David had difficulty believing Rediscover would rely solely on a new recruit to swipe research data. There would be backup.

"I need you to stay on your toes in the neighborhood and at the hospital," Casey instructed.

"Always."

"If you spot him, notify us immediately. In the meantime, I'll expect regular updates."

"Yes, sir."

The call ended and David was alone with his laptop once more. He pinched the bridge of his nose. He didn't want to stalk Terri. He wanted to pry into the raw emotional wounds even less, but he needed a better read on who Trey had been. Worse, he needed it yesterday.

He couldn't blame himself for not knowing

more already. He'd only been on the job for a few weeks, but peeling back the layers of a personal life packed with tragedy required a deft touch. Damn. David wasn't sure how to push any harder without blowing it all to hell.

It was too late to back down, too late to realize he wasn't up to the task. He had the strangest urge to ask his mom for advice. There was no easy way to do that, either, even if he changed names and modified the facts. Calling for advice on a woman would only raise more questions and mess up Terri's potential Christmas visit. Assuming, if he had to take down her brother, she still wanted anything to do with him.

Growing up, he'd known he had a good family. The Martins were stable and happy, with no more theatrics than three older sisters normally provided. His parents had raised four children to become self-sufficient and contributing members of society. He knew that wasn't always the case. It seemed the farther he traveled, the more he saw, the more he appreciated all the little things that had come together to give him the right start.

He stood up to stretch, then paced between the kitchen and den, wishing for a pool.

Terri spoke of her family in similar terms, with plenty of love and affection under the sadness. The background the Specialists had pulled on her brother pointed to a decent kid who'd gone off track four years ago, right after the accident.

Why had he snapped? Wandering away from college after everything Terri had done for him? In David's book that was nearly unforgivable.

Dropping back into the chair, he went through Trey Barnhart's background once more, doing his best to view it objectively rather than through the lens of his instinctive protectiveness of a friend. Trey had played sports through high school. Not a star in the classroom, but he wasn't a slouch, either. He'd taken tougher science classes while doing well enough in the basic requirements on the English and history side.

The medical file after the car accident wasn't pretty. He'd been banged up, his knees and ankles damaged enough to end his hope of riding a baseball scholarship through college. David had watched friends deal with similar problems. Life was full of disappointment. Most people found a way to cope, overcome or move on. Sure there were scars, surgical and otherwise, but that was part of growing up. Terri had managed to keep going. Why hadn't Trey followed her example?

It could be timing. A shrink would likely blame it on emotional development or birth order. Trey had suffered a significant loss on several levels at the wrong life stage or he'd been coddled as the youngest and the pile of challenges proved too much for him.

David snarled. He wasn't a shrink, he was an operative. He wanted actionable points he could work with to prevent an attack. What message had Rediscover used, assuming Casey was right about Trey's involvement, to turn him against the core values of his childhood?

No answers, clear or otherwise, were forthcoming. David checked his surveillance equipment. Everything was quiet in Terri's house. Frustrated, he powered down the laptop and headed upstairs for bed.

Whatever Trey was into—willing or coerced—if he showed up and gave Terri trouble, David vowed to adjust the kid's attitude about family, respect and gratitude.

TERRI PRACTICALLY FLOATED through the kitchen, packing her lunch with more muscle memory than conscious thought. That task complete, she hurried upstairs to get ready for bed. Her alarm would go off in just over five hours and she owed it to her patients to be rested and ready.

Rest wasn't going to happen, she realized with a silly smile. Her mind kept drifting off task as she went through her bedtime routine. She had to check the calendar several times before she managed to lay out the right color scrubs for the morning, and then she picked up the moisturizer instead of her makeup remover. She almost squeezed her tube of eye cream onto her toothbrush. Good grief, she hadn't been this distracted over a kiss since high school.

Shaking her head at her dreamy-eyed reflection, she told herself to get it together. This was a serious overreaction to a sweet, simple kiss. It had been a friendly gesture, possibly even a joke. Had they ever decided if the evening was actually a date?

She slid into the soft oversize T-shirt she wore as a nightgown and flopped into bed. Snuggling under the covers, she closed her eyes and remembered David's face. His tender lips. His masculine scent. His deep laughter.

Who was she kidding? She wasn't going to get any sleep without drastic action. Sitting up, she plumped the pillows and flipped on the bedside lamp. Picking up the medical journal she'd left on her nightstand, she started reading. Surely research stats and control groups would have her snoozing in no time.

The magazine slipped from her relaxed fingers as she started to doze until a sound brought her wide-awake. She clutched the magazine tight and tried to pinpoint the source as she waited to hear it again, praying she was wrong.

She wasn't. The hinges on the screen door at

the back of the house whined again. Her heart raced. Someone was trying to get inside her house.

Before she could decide on a weapon, a firm knock echoed through the house. She swallowed back the surge of fear, knowing it was natural. Living alone rarely bothered her, but then again, no one had ever knocked on her door at this hour. She grabbed the handset for the landline, a holdover habit from her parents, and tiptoed down the stairs in the dark. She peered around the corner as another knock rattled the hinges. She'd already dialed 9 and 1 when the person outside called out.

"Come on, Terri. Wake up already."

Trey's voice. Her brother was back! Shock was quickly followed by relief, with anger running a close third. Her mind and body couldn't agree on what to do first. She turned off the phone and hurried through the kitchen, flipping on the light. The tile was cold under her bare feet as she approached the door, giving chilly reassurance this wasn't some strange dream or terrible nightmare.

"It's me, Terri!" Trey called through the door. "Let me in."

On a silent prayer of gratitude, she unlocked the door and jumped back as Trey rushed inside. He threw his arms around her and gave her a rib-crushing hug. Patting his shoulder awkwardly, she wondered where to begin.

"You're alive." She stepped back and stared at him. "You're alive…" She repeated the obvious while she cataloged the changes. His skin was tanned to a golden glow, reminding her of the summers he'd worked as a lifeguard at the water park. He seemed taller, which she supposed was possible, though it probably had more to do with his straight posture and clearly improved fitness. When they'd moved him into college, he was on the skinny side of healthy. Now he'd filled out, looking more like a man in his prime. "Did you join the military?"

"Like they'd take me," he said with a dry laugh. He shrugged off his backpack and dropped it by the door. Moving past her, he opened a cabinet and pulled out a drinking glass.

It was the laughter and his familiarity with the kitchen that snapped her out of the relieved haze and had her temper flaring. She closed and locked the door, giving herself a moment to grab back control. Didn't work. "Where the hell have you been?"

"That didn't take long," he replied, pulling the water pitcher out of the refrigerator.

Terri had never been so furious with him. She should be happy, delighted to see him safe and whole. Part of her was, but it was buried under a blaze of anger. Her vision hazed red at the edges, and she laced her fingers together to keep from slapping that bitter smirk right off his face. He wasn't showing an ounce of remorse for what he'd put her through.

All her sacrifice to cover his college, all her effort and energy to get him healthy, and he just walked away. Without a word. "Get out."

"What? I just got *back*."

"Get out." She unlocked the door and jerked it open once more. "I'm not letting you do this to me." She had her pride and a newfound sense of self-preservation. She wouldn't let him tear that apart.

"You haven't given me a chance to explain."

"Why should I?" She clamped her mouth shut before she said something she'd regret. The insults and accusations eager to break free were only manifestations of her battered feelings. Striking out wouldn't fix anything and could hurt them both in the long run. "You owe me an apology first," she said, managing to stay calm. "Do it right and maybe I'll listen to your explanation." If he did it wrong, she could call Suzette and watch her friend rip into him. It was a powerfully satisfying image.

"Okay," he replied. "Can we close the door?"

"As long as we're clear that you can't stay here."

"Come on," he sputtered. "This is my home, too."

"Actually, it's not." She planted her hands on her hips. "Not legally." A gush of resentment swamped her. "Where the hell have you been?"

"I—"

"I hired a private investigator to look for you!"

"Terri—"

"You disappeared," she interrupted again. "Not a word for three months!"

"I'm sorry." He held up his hands. "It wasn't about you. It was—"

"Oh, no. Try again. You should know it's going to take more than that."

"I'm sorry," he said quietly. "Really sorry. Disappearing was selfish."

"Cruel."

He frowned at her, clearly baffled by the exchange. "Not intentionally."

She crossed her arms over her chest and leveled a glare at him, that image of Suzette hauling him to the curb firmly in her mind.

"Come on, sis. I needed space," he said. "Arizona gave me that. We talked about it."

"We talked about college," she snapped.

"I know. It was great at first. Then classes got ramped up and it was too much. An overload. I'm sorry I left you hanging—"

"You left me worried to death. For months."

"—and worried," he added, bobbing his head in agreement. "You have to realize what a mess I was. I needed to get my mind straight."

"What?" She couldn't believe this crap he was shoveling at her. "You were pretty squared away on move-in day. Before that, actually."

His gaze hit the floor. "I wanted you to think so."

"No." She shook her head. "Don't even try to pin this on me. You are utterly immovable when you want to be." She wagged a finger at him. "No one forced you to complete those applications. Northern Arizona was your decision. If I'd had a choice you would've gone to Clemson or USC."

He swore. "That would've been worse. All my friends are upperclassmen. The teams—"

She'd believed for years that he would outgrow his selfish streak. "You suck at apologies, Trey." She picked up the phone, tapping it against her palm. "Get on with your explanation before I call the police. Or worse."

"Who would be worse than the cops?"

"Suzette."

"Oh, God." His eyes went wide and the words tumbled out. "I wanted something different. You know I needed a fresh start."

"Old news." She'd heard this when he was applying to various schools.

"I know." He took a breath. "I liked college. My roommate was great. I had a few friends, but I was older."

And still so immature. By some miracle those words stayed in her head. The dorm had been her only option financially and though she'd never said it, she'd thought the community and structure of dorm life were a good idea. It might've been different if he'd stayed in state and chosen to room with reliable friends.

"I got involved and connected with various groups on campus. Even the intramural softball team. One group was awesome. They had dinners and gave some pitches about self-improvement. You wouldn't believe how effective they are. The people I met liked me, too. They talked to me about the process and offered me some really cool options that included a decent job."

"Cool options like dropping out and not having the decency to make a phone call to your only sister?"

"I honestly thought I could get through the first phase before you knew what happened."

The first phase? "Gee, thanks for that."

"Seriously," he insisted. "My plan was to call right away, but the process took longer for me. I had some issues."

He had issues all right. They both did. "What process?" It was starting to sound like he'd joined a cult. She shook off the disturbing thought. Cults typically didn't allow people to leave whenever they wanted.

"The first phase is like a mental clearinghouse and physical boot camp at the same time. It's team policy for everyone they hire."

"What kind of team?" If he had a job, they'd given him a new bank account. She managed the one here for him and hadn't seen anything other than his first work-study pay come through.

"Company is too formal." He grinned at her. "They get picky about the terms and phrasing to keep up productivity. Anyway, the goal is to purge the past in order to move forward with purpose."

"How so?" Every word out of his mouth raised more questions. She wanted names and contact information so she could check it out. This felt wrong.

"Meditation," he said, rolling his eyes. "It's so much tougher than it sounds."

She nodded her agreement and felt herself smiling a little. Sitting still had never been Trey's strong suit.

"I didn't mean to worry you or cause you any stress. I just wanted to get square." He cleared his throat and studied his shoes. "Being away made the nightmares worse. I had to do something."

He made a valid point, whether she liked it or not. She understood the heartache and sorrow that fueled those nightmares and she hadn't been in the car. "Your counselor warned you that was possible. Likely."

"I know," he admitted.

"There were plenty of options that didn't include dropping out," she said.

He met her gaze, his eyes brittle and his jaw set in a stubborn line. "I chose the best option available for me at the time."

She nodded grudgingly. He said all the right words, but she was either too tired or too angry to accept them. His reappearance and flood of unanswered questions drained her. She didn't want to fight about what couldn't be changed now. She glanced at the clock, suddenly exhausted. "I want to hear more about it, but not tonight." Tomorrow was going to be impossible if she didn't get some sleep. "I have to be up and ready to work in a few hours."

"You're going in?"

"Yes." Did he expect her to stay home?

"I thought we could spend some time together."

"And we will," she promised. She gave him a hug, then walked toward the stairs, pausing when he followed her. "After my shift we can hammer out the details about you staying here, if that's what you have in mind."

He scowled at her. "What else would I have in mind? The team is letting me telecommute for up to a month for the holidays to make amends and reconnect. They value family. You're my sister. This is home. Where else would I go?"

She ran her hand over the smooth wood of the banister. "Accepting your apology and explanation doesn't just erase everything I've gone through while you were finding yourself. My house, my rules." She swallowed, hating the words she had to say and the conflicted feelings swirling through her. "I'm not sure I'm comfortable with you living here."

"Some homecoming," he grumbled. "I shouldn't have to earn the right to live at home with my sister."

Although she felt confident he sincerely believed he had made smart choices for himself, she didn't trust herself around him yet. His disappearance had crushed her and she couldn't leave herself open to more of that pain. "If you wanted a parade, you should've given me some notice," she snapped. She struggled to be fair, to treat him as she'd want to be treated. "I'm glad you've found yourself and work you enjoy. Honestly, I'm overjoyed to see you and pleased that you came in person to make amends. Your happiness matters to me and it always will. If you want to rebuild our relationship, you can start by showing some of that newfound maturity by acknowledging that my feelings matter, too."

His face fell and he looked instantly ashamed. "You're right. I'm just tired."

She reached out and gave him a hug. For a moment it felt like old times when they'd settled a fight and Mom urged them to hug and make up. "We'll both feel better tomorrow."

When she crawled back into bed, her brain didn't want to rest. She closed her eyes, hoping that would be enough. She was beyond the ability of the medical journal to bore her to sleep and she'd never been any good at meditation, either. Still, she tried, focusing on her breathing, on letting everything slide away.

It had been a roller-coaster night from her fun maybe-a-date to that soft kiss to her brother's surprise arrival. Tempting as it was, she wouldn't call in sick tomorrow. It was the last day of her rotation and she needed the work to distract her and give her a break from her suddenly complicated personal life.

Chapter Five

Thanks to hefty doses of caffeine and only a handful of patients on the ward, the first half of Terri's shift went smoothly. It would change as patients started moving up from post-op recovery. Terri didn't mind—the action would keep her awake and on her game until her shift ended.

On her break, she carried her lunch downstairs to the cafeteria, hoping to run into David without being obvious about it. Instead, she bumped into her dear friend Dr. Palmer. He gave her a big hug and then, missing nothing, pointed out the dark circles under her eyes.

"Are you feeling well?"

"Just didn't manage much sleep last night," she replied, making a mental note to find a better concealer.

"Have the nightmares returned?"

"No." He was like a father to her and yet she'd

never confided to him that Trey had gone missing. At first because she was sure her brother would turn up again soon. Then, as the weeks had dragged on, it felt too much like a failure. She'd considered telling Franklin when the PI came up empty, but she didn't want to get him involved. "Trey got in late and we were talking."

"Ah." He pulled out a chair for her. "How was his first semester?"

"Eventful," she hedged. "Would you expect anything else from Trey?"

"I suppose not."

Franklin laughed and the jovial, booming sound erased part of her lingering tension. This man had become her lifeline when she needed both career and personal support right out of nursing school. They'd met when he was a patient and she answered a call in his room, unaware he was a VIP around here. The charge nurse on the shift had been livid when Terri, the least experienced of the nurses on the ward, exercised initiative. She'd drafted a reprimand immediately and Terri could've lost her job. The job she needed to take care of her brother and his mounting medical expenses. Her parents' life insurance had paid off the mortgage and cars, but it hadn't left much in the way of an inheritance.

Franklin had liked her instantly and made no

secret about his preference for her ability and bedside manner. He got the reprimand tossed out before it landed in Terri's permanent record. He'd even hired her as a private nurse when he was discharged. Those extra shifts had made it possible to fund her brother's education.

"What are you doing down here?" she asked, pushing Trey to the back of her mind for the moment.

"I have a patient upstairs and I was looking for you."

"How come?" She hoped he had some interesting case to discuss, or even another private nursing job for her to consider. She needed the distraction.

"We haven't talked in some time. I've missed you."

"Two weeks, maybe," she teased. Opening her lunch bag, she popped open her bowl of salad greens. "What's new?"

He leaned forward, his eyes sparkling. "You first. A little bird told me you had a date last night."

So that was why he'd sought her out. "Please. You never listen to the gossips." She stuffed a big bite of salad into her mouth to buy a little time to find a good answer.

"Avoidance." He winked. "The gossip must be true."

"Not in the way you're implying." She shook her head. "I went out—just as friends—with David Martin from HR. We had a fun time."

Franklin's eyebrows arched. "Friends," he echoed. "You need more than that."

"Pardon me?" She wasn't sure why Franklin was suddenly interested in her social life.

"Fun is a good start, but you deserve more."

"Maybe I'm not ready for more." She poked at her salad, all too eager to confide in someone who wouldn't immediately start making wedding plans. Talking with Trey wasn't an option, leaving Franklin as the closest thing she had to family. "I admit it would be easy to think of David as someone more than a friend." She paused, her mind drifting back to that wonderful kiss.

"So why not see where that path leads?"

"I've always believed it's best to take things slow." With her brother back in town and eager to reconnect, slow was the only option. "He just moved to Charleston."

"I bet he admires our wonderful views. What did you do last night?"

She smiled. "We had dinner downtown and then caught Battery Lane at Benny's." She knew her expression had gone dreamy when Franklin grinned. "We walked along the seawall before he took me home."

"My wife always delighted in the holiday displays."

There was the catalyst. Franklin was feeling sentimental. She could certainly understand that, especially this time of year. "It was lovely," she agreed.

"He sounds like a smart boy," Franklin added.

"Man," she corrected automatically. Trey was a boy. Despite the emotional and physical growth, the difference had been alarmingly clear to her last night. "David is a smart *man*."

"I see."

"No, you just think you do," she said, digging into her salad again.

"I'm allowed to want the best for you. Maybe I'll swing by his department and introduce myself."

She wasn't sure how David would take such a dadlike move. "Friends," she reminded Franklin in a hurry. "Neither of us wants to rush into serious territory."

Franklin frowned. "Why not? Life is short, Terri. A smart man is one who sees your value. He should want to be serious about you."

"Thanks?" This was quickly moving past simple holiday sentimentalism. She and Franklin had spent hours talking during his recovery, and he'd listened to her ramble about losing her parents and caring for Trey and struggling to balance all the new responsibility in her life. He'd even given her legal advice in addition to everything else. Without Franklin, she could easily have lost everything in that first year, including her sanity. "Where is this coming from?"

"It's been four *years*, Terri. You've been in a holding pattern, doing what is required but not living to the fullest. With good reason, of course," he added when she started to interrupt. "Trey is healthy and on his own at school much of the year. You have time for yourself. I want to know you're living. I want to see you happy."

Her eyes welled at his concern. She wanted to blame the reaction on her lack of sleep, but that wouldn't be fair. Being loved, feeling cared for was something she missed. Without Franklin, she wasn't sure she'd remember what it felt like at all.

"Tell me about him," Franklin suggested.

"David is all about the water," she began. "He grew up on the Georgia coast. He's scuba certified. He used to lead underwater tours. He worked with the Coast Guard before coming to MUSC."

"Does he have family?"

She grinned, thinking of David's sisters. "He's the youngest, with three older sisters. They drive him bonkers with blind dates every time he goes home for a weekend."

"I'm starting to wonder why he left the Coast Guard."

"I thought the same thing after he told me some of the wilder stories. His sisters really want him settled down."

Franklin's eyes went misty. "Family is important, as we both know."

"It's the rock we're all built on," she agreed, quoting one of his favorite sayings and making him smile. "I'm glad we have each other," Terri said softly, reaching across to pat his hand.

Franklin might have filled her father's shoes, but she knew she'd filled a void for him, as well. He'd lost his wife years ago to cancer, and his daughter had died early, too, though Franklin never discussed the circumstances. There were a few formal portraits he kept around the house, but that seemed the extent of his ability to share. Terri didn't press the issue, well aware that he would tell her someday when he couldn't bear the burden alone any longer.

Franklin cleared his throat and took a sip from his coffee. "Aside from the chatter of little birds, there is another reason I wanted to speak with you."

She arched her eyebrows, waiting.

"I wanted you on the care team for my patient, but the timing didn't work out."

"That's okay." She smiled. "I'm past the stage where I need the extra shifts just to get by."

"That's good news," he replied. "At this stage, my patient will get bored quickly waiting for test results. He could use your company if you have time."

She was immediately curious about the situation, but she knew better than to ask outside of his office. Many of his projects were sensitive, proprietary developments. "I'm happy to stop by and say hello."

"I appreciate that. I'll get your name on the visitors' list as soon as I'm back upstairs."

Terri smiled. Dr. Palmer was a rock star in the biotech field, and getting into his ward when he had a patient was often like gaining access to a hot nightclub in New York.

Franklin slid out of the booth. "Now I must drop in on a certain new employee in HR."

Terri laughed. "If you scare him away…" Franklin could be more than a little intimidating when he wanted to be.

"Then we'll know for sure he wasn't good enough for you."

"Ha-ha. Just play nice," she warned.

"You have my word," he replied, giving her shoulder a squeeze as he left.

Terri finished her lunch, her mind on the family she'd started with and the family of friends she was building. Change was an inevitable part of life and for the first time in a long while, she wasn't afraid of what new surprise was waiting around the corner.

When she returned to her floor, the spring in her step faded as all eyes turned her way. It seemed everyone was gathered near the nurses station. Waiting for her. "What's wrong?"

"Not a single thing." Janet beamed at her and pointed to a lush bouquet filling the space between two monitors. "Those just arrived from Flower Ever After. For *you*."

"Oh." It was all she could manage. The florist on King Street was considered one of the best in the area for any occasion. A frosted glass vase in pale pink anchored an exquisite arrangement of pale white lilies, bright tulips and deep glossy holly.

"Go on, open the card."

"Right." Her hand shook as she reached for the small white envelope, trying to keep her expectations in check. It was clear that "little bird" had told quite a few people about her possibly-a-date last night, but this was likely Trey's way of sucking up rather than a romantic gesture from David.

She couldn't hold back the smile as she read the brief message in David's handwriting:

To chase away first date jitters.
—David.

"Well?" Janet clearly spoke for the entire group staring at her. "It's from the new hunk in HR, isn't it?"

She laughed. The nickname given to David was too ridiculous. Fitting but ridiculous. "Yes."

"Give us details."

"No," Terri said, burying her nose in the soft fragrance of the cheerful flowers. "We have patients to take care of."

"One detail," Janet begged, leading a chorus of agreement.

Terri pretended to think about it. "Two details." Everyone's eyes lit up. "He's a perfect gentleman," she said, ignoring the ensuing groans. "And that new mac-and-cheese place on King Street is fabulous."

She shooed them all back to work and tucked the card into her pocket, not wanting to let it out of her sight. What did it mean that he'd written the note himself rather than just call in an order? With the sweet scent of the lilies tickling her nose, she warned herself not to read too much between the lines of what appeared to be a romantic gesture.

Rushing headlong into something serious could break their friendship, and that was the last thing she wanted.

DAVID HAD HAD better days. He'd slept fitfully, dreaming of Terri. Giving up on sleep, he'd rolled out of bed for an early workout. After he'd showered and dressed, with his first cup of coffee in hand, he checked the bugs at the Barnhart place. Hearing the unmistakable return of Terri's brother, he'd nearly choked.

Casey's team was already analyzing every word the bugs had caught, and David had known it was time to up his game. He ordered the flowers for Terri on his way to work and then had been caught up in meetings all day. Her shift would be over in less than two hours. Sketchy brother or not, he'd had a good time last night, and after that kiss sending flowers seemed like the right thing to do. He didn't want to come off as overeager, but he didn't want her thinking he was a jerk, either. At least not any sooner than necessary.

He'd barely settled at his desk when the text alert came through that Dr. Palmer had admitted his patient for a procedure earlier this morning. It put him in full agreement with the analysts that Trey's return to the States at this time was no coincidence. The doctor's research wasn't widely publicized, making David wonder how Rediscover had known when to send Trey in.

If he could just get upstairs to see Terri. It would be nice to know if she liked the flowers, but he really wanted firsthand assurance that she was okay with Trey's return. Although the HR post kept him busy, the lack of a physical challenge gave him far too much time to think about the potential threats and the woman who might be unknowingly caught up in a problem beyond her comprehension.

He was almost antsy by the time he was finally able to get a few minutes away from his desk. It was impossible not to think about what kind of reaction was waiting for him upstairs. Maybe flowers had been a mistake. He didn't want her booting him to the curb right when Casey needed him to stick close.

Reminding himself of his primary job, David swung by the security desk and said hello to a couple of guys he played racquetball with. It gave him an excuse to make sure everything was running smoothly in and around the hospital. With nothing obviously out of place, he headed for the main lobby elevators to check on Terri. He planned to walk the corridors near Palmer's research wing on his way back to his desk.

When the elevator arrived, David stepped inside, along with several other people, and asked for Terri's floor. When he looked up, Trey was jogging to catch the same car. The person closest to the buttons held the door, and David shifted back to make more room. Trey checked the lit buttons and faced the closing doors without requesting another floor. David wasn't surprised he was going to see his sister and he was relieved Trey hadn't pushed the number for Palmer's floor.

In the polite hush, David studied Trey. Either the file had been out-of-date, or he had been working out—hard—while he was off the radar. David reluctantly gave him credit for regaining the athleticism the accident had stolen.

When the doors parted on Terri's floor, Trey exited quickly and turned for the nurses station. David waited until the last moment, then stepped out and turned down the hall in the opposite direction. He cut through the central patient lounge, coming at the nurses station from the reverse side. He leaned against the wall outside a patient's room and pulled out his phone. He sent a text message to the director while he listened, hoping to get a better sense of how things were between the Barnhart siblings.

"Is Terri here?" David heard Trey ask. Did he really believe surprising her at work was a good idea? Based on the little his bugs had caught last night, David didn't think so.

"Well, well. Trey Barnhart, as I live and breathe."

David peeked around the corner at the new voice. Terri's friend Suzette was advancing on Trey, her face fierce and angry. "What are you doing here?"

"Hi, Suzette. I'm home for the break and—"

"Don't you lie to me." Suzette jerked him toward the small kitchen behind the nurses station, and David lost the rest of the conversation. The body language told a pretty clear story. Suzette had Trey pinned back against the glass wall and was reading him the riot act. Apparently Terri had confided in Suzette about her brother's disappearance.

When Suzette allowed Trey to leave the kitchen, his face was flushed. His hands fisted at his sides and he was clearly struggling for self-control.

"Wait here," Suzette ordered Trey. "I'll find her."

"I'm not going anywhere."

Suzette snorted. "Give me a reason to call Security," she challenged.

David seconded that statement, studying Trey as Suzette went to find Terri. He wasn't happy about the delay or interference, but he was pulling himself together. Before David could scold himself for wanting the brother to make a mistake, Terri was hurrying toward him.

"What are you doing here?" she asked.

He gave her points for composure, though he could see the tension in the set of her mouth and the small furrow between her eyebrows.

"I thought we could have lunch."

"I've already been to lunch. You should've called," Terri replied.

"Come on, give me five minutes. Someone can cover while we grab a coffee, right?"

Alarms went off in David's head. Had Trey already put something in motion for Rediscover? Was he trying to get Terri out of the way?

"No. Thank you," she added. "I'll be home right after shift."

"Which ends when?" Trey asked, exasperated.

"Three at the earliest." She glanced around. "You need to go. I thought you said you were working today."

David made mental notes to piece together this chat with the conversation the bugs had picked up last night. Hopefully, the team could come up with a working theory.

"Telecommuting." He shrugged. "I set my own hours."

Cocky, David thought, his irritation mounting. "Lucky you."

"That's right," Trey agreed. "It's a good job and I have a purpose. Isn't that what you said you always wanted for me?"

David gritted his teeth as Terri nodded her agreement.

"That doesn't mean you can waltz in here," she warned, "whenever you want and put my job at risk."

"As if you don't have the right connections to smooth over any trouble," Trey challenged.

That was pushing the line. David's irritation inched closer to anger. If Trey had been like this frequently, Terri deserved a medal for not leaving him to fend for himself. After everything Terri had done, she didn't deserve this crap from the only family she had left.

"You need to leave now," Terri said, backing away from her brother. "I need to get back to my patients."

"I can't believe you won't make time for me," Trey grumbled. "Are those flowers for you?"

"No," she answered quickly. "A patient was discharged before they arrived."

"You're lying."

And David wondered why. Trey's snide laughter scraped at his nerves.

"That's why you don't want me in the house. I'll get between you and whoever you're banging." He laughed again. "You weren't worried at all."

David's hands clenched and it took all his control to stay out of it.

"That's enough," Terri said in her brisk, official voice. "I don't have time to convince you otherwise, Trey. Thanks for stopping by. I'll see you at home."

"Sure." Trey shoved his hands deep into his pockets and stalked toward the elevator.

David was torn. He needed to follow Trey—and he would—but Terri looked upset. He counted to three and rounded the corner, sending her a warm smile when her eyes landed on him.

"Hey," he said, pretending he'd missed that train wreck. "You like the flowers?" He tipped his head toward the arrangement behind her.

"They're beautiful." She glanced around, saw they were alone and reached across the desk, giving his hand a quick squeeze. "Thank you. I'd chat more, but I—" her gaze slid toward the elevators and back "—I'm running behind."

"Can I see you tonight?"

"I'd like that…"

"But?"

She motioned him toward the kitchen and a bit more privacy. "Trey came home."

"What?" Inwardly, David breathed a sigh of relief that she'd told him right away. He didn't have real cause to doubt her, but it made him feel better that she trusted him. "When?"

"Late last night," she said on a sigh. "Total surprise. I can't get into all of it right now. He looks good," she said. "In fact, you just missed him."

"Huh." David crossed his arms over his chest. "Are you okay? Did he tell you where he's been?"

"I'm not sure I'm all right, but I am relieved," she admitted.

"You don't look it."

"It's just—well…" She rubbed the back of her hand across her forehead. "It's complicated. Let me spend tonight catching up with my brother. I'll text you."

"Do that. Whatever you need, Terri, count on me."

Her eyes went soft. "Thank you."

"Take care," he said as they parted ways.

David didn't like this. It might have been unprofessional to put Terri's feelings ahead of the mission, but he didn't regret it. He told himself he'd been verifying that she wasn't willingly tangled up with Trey's problems. Taking the elevator back to the main lobby, David walked a circuit of the public area. Not seeing Trey, he returned to his desk and used his access to check out the security feed for any sign of the brother on the hospital grounds.

He picked up someone who resembled Trey heading for the parking garage, and David kept moving through the various camera views to track his progress. There. Trey had gone to the parking garage all right, then back into the hospital through the outpatient entrance.

"What the hell are you up to?" David muttered at the screen as he watched Trey enter an elevator heading down. He couldn't think of any reason Trey would need to be in the morgue, which was the only hospital department in the basement. Determined to head off a problem, David left his desk to get eyes on Trey.

Chapter Six

David took the stairs two at a time down to the morgue level. If he was lucky, he'd catch Trey causing trouble. The morgue was in the original part of the building. He was betting Trey didn't know there was only one way out that wouldn't trip alarms and have the Charleston Police Department flooding the hospital campus.

He stepped out of the stairwell, easing the door closed so it wouldn't slam and tip Trey off. He heard the distinct squeak of shoes on the industrial flooring and followed the sounds.

What could Trey want down here?

David's research of MUSC had begun with his training for the HR position, before he'd left the Specialist headquarters. He'd learned the location of every department and lab, and since he'd been on site, he'd personally discovered every shortcut, corner and error on the building plans.

He heard a door slam farther along the hallway and skidded to a stop. That wasn't the morgue.

The morgue door had been replaced with a secure electronic system. The only other destinations down here were service areas for power, maintenance and infrastructure.

David swore, moving with more care toward the service access doors, doors that would slam. If he rushed inside, it would be too easy for the brother to get by him and escape. At his current position, he could still cut off Trey if he tried to get back to the main hospital levels.

Suddenly the lights went out. The hallway was nothing more than a black tunnel with vague glowing smudges from the emergency exit signs. His heart rate picking up, David put his back to the nearest wall and waited. The generators would kick on soon to power safety lighting throughout the hospital as well as the essential medical equipment for patients upstairs.

As part of orientation, every hospital employee was trained for various types of emergencies from a localized fire to a terrorist attack. Too bad David didn't know which end of the emergency scale he was dealing with down here.

Trey didn't emerge, but David wasn't ready to give up his post covering the only logical escape route.

David squinted into the darkness and held his breath to listen for other sounds. If the generators had kicked in, he couldn't hear them, and no lights in this area recovered. His gut went cold. To cut both the main power and the redundancy precautions would take a coordinated strike and more than one person.

He heard the squeak of shoes and pressed back against the wall. A shape loped through the gloom, heading directly for the stairwell. It could only be Trey. Sirens were audible now, even down here. Soon, the hospital would be crawling with police and other personnel eager to sort out the problem. David just had to keep Trey from escaping.

He leaped out as Trey passed him, driving him into the opposite wall. The air rushed out of his lungs with a loud *oof.* David dodged Trey's effort to block him, and his fist glanced off a dark knit mask covering his face. That seemed like an excessive precaution considering the lack of light.

David tugged at the mask while Trey squirmed, though it was still too dark to make a positive ID. He wanted to pound him for causing trouble, despite the potential of breaking his hand if he missed and hit the concrete wall. He jerked Trey back to the center of the hallway and spun him around. Pushing at the back of his knee, he planned to pin him until the lights came back on.

Trey had other ideas. Curling into a ball, he rolled out of reach. David lunged and caught a fist full of fabric. He yanked, but Trey shook him off and left him with a useless jacket. What he wouldn't give for better lighting. His best option was to get the guy turned around and hope he ran the wrong way.

David went on the offensive, diving low for the guy's shoes. He caught him at the knee and took a heel to the ribs. In or out of water, David knew how to regulate his breathing. He scrambled for a better angle to get him down again. In the dark, he tripped over the coat. Picking it up, he leaped and wrapped it over Trey's head.

The younger man fought to get the jacket off his face. He stumbled backward, his voice muffled but the nature of the language clear enough as he used his body to pin David to the wall. David held on like a sandbur, pulling the jacket tight around his face until his body went slack and his knees buckled.

"What the hell are you up to, Trey?" he asked as he eased his limp body toward the floor.

And where the hell were the generators? He could hear alarms and sirens, even shouts from the staff caught in the morgue, but he didn't hear generators.

The timing of Trey's return and today's visit wasn't coincidental. With his knee in Trey's back, he eased the jacket off his head and reached for the mask once more. He'd take a picture with his phone and then the authorities would have something to work with.

His hand closed over his phone, but he didn't get it out of his pocket before he heard another footfall behind him. He twisted around, unable to hang on to his prisoner and still avoid an attack. A hard blow landed against his head.

David fell back, covering his head against another blow as lights danced across his vision, if not the corridor. He struggled to his knees, desperate to catch one of the men responsible for cutting off the power supply. He heard the clang of metal and the slap of the security bar on the stairwell door. His best effort wasn't going to be enough. He swore as the two men reached the stairwell before he could regain his footing.

UPSTAIRS, TERRI WAS making her final rounds with patients. In less than an hour she'd hand off the ward to the next shift. Most days the end-of-shift tasks gave her a sense of pride and accomplishment. Today, she couldn't drum up as much enthusiasm. She felt like the worst sort of hypocrite because she was eager to go visit Franklin's patient but had no desire to go home and talk to her brother, who'd been missing for months.

She glanced at the beautiful flowers on the desk, wishing for some guarantee that Trey would keep his mouth shut about her social life.

The fact that he didn't have the right to say anything never seemed to stop him. On a sigh, she took a picture with her phone. She had the card David had written in her pocket. It might be a silly cop-out, but she'd print the snapshot and put it on her vanity mirror with the card as a reminder her moody brother couldn't tarnish. She didn't want Trey to have one more excuse to avoid the real issue of where he'd been all this time and what he planned to do next.

Suddenly the power went out and the ward went silent. For a few seconds no one spoke, and then voices—some scared, others reassuring—filled the void. They had plenty of afternoon light pouring through the windows and she counted that a blessing as she shifted into the emergency protocol.

They didn't have any crisis patients. The biggest concerns, if the outage lasted any length of time, would be keeping the powered cooling packs going and the children calm.

Terri called out to the rest of her staff and got the visual and verbal assurance they were all okay. "Generators should be up shortly," she said as she walked along. "Get everyone into their rooms. We have batteries for IV pumps and you all know how to do vitals the old-school way."

They disappeared in a flurry of action while she returned to the desk. She picked up a phone to call security, forgetting it wasn't battery operated. She reached for the radio, instead, hoping to hear something helpful. What she heard was chaos.

Turning down the volume, she decided her ward wouldn't contribute to the overwhelmed security and support staff. The benefit of a pediatric ward was the cheerful decor and the upbeat attitude. And the low crisis risk, she added when she heard alarms sounding on the floor above them. Fear clogged her throat for a moment when she remembered that Franklin's research ward and special patient were up there.

Where the hell were the generators?

She made another circuit, reassuring parents and patients that the power glitch would be resolved quickly and no evacuation order had been issued. If she had any kind of good luck, she'd get a report from Security before one of the children or parents picked up a rumor on their cell phones.

Her luck held up, as did her patients, with a good dose of humor and understanding. Still, it was the longest two hours of her professional life before the ward started to hum again with computers and equipment as the power was gradually restored to each floor. She was rebooting their system when the elevators started functioning and someone from Security appeared along with the next shift of nurses.

"We're all set," she said to the guard. "Do you have any idea what happened?"

"It's not clear yet," he said, pitching his voice low. "I'm here about your car."

"My car?"

"Yes, ma'am." He turned an iPad her way, and she gasped at the picture. "Several cars were vandalized during the power outage."

Remembering where she was, Terri bit back the colorful curse on the tip of her tongue. "Great. Do I need to file a police report?"

"We have that started for you downstairs. Please stop by the security desk on your way home."

"I will. Thank you." Somehow, she managed to get through the shift change without giving in to the primal urge to scream in frustration. How was she going to get home?

It wasn't easy to stay calm as she stood at the security desk trying to figure out the next step. Her car was part of a collective crime scene. Once the crime team was done, the vehicles would be available to be claimed for repairs. Sometime tomorrow. Maybe. Terri rolled her shoulders, trying to shed some of the building tension. In her case, she needed two new tires, a new side mirror and a new rear bumper. The pictures of such senseless damage shocked her.

"They don't have any suspects?"

The guard shook his head. "The guy dodged the camera angles. Should I call a cab for you?"

"No, thanks. I'll call my…" She pulled out her phone and started dialing before she remembered she didn't have a valid number for her brother. The cell phone she'd been paying for had been left in his dorm room with his other personal belongings. She started to dial the house phone, then stopped. This was an emotional no-win situation. If he didn't answer, she'd be irritated with him for not waiting for her at the house. If he did answer, what could he do? He didn't have a car. Even if he found a way to help her out, she'd be opening herself up for heartache as soon as he left again. "Please call a cab."

"Don't bother. I'll take her home."

Terri swiveled around at the sound of David's voice. His easy smile radiated calm and confidence. Two things she needed extra doses of at the moment.

"If that's okay with you?" he asked, patting her gently on the shoulder. "I saw your car on the police report."

"You did?" How had he heard before she did?

"They mentioned your car and I was concerned," he said. "Ready?"

"More than." As much as she loved her job, she was ready for her forty-eight hours off. "It's been a tough day." And it wasn't over. Trey would be waiting for her at home.

She wanted to believe that would go well, but after the past few hours, she was more exhausted than she'd been last night. Unfortunately, she wouldn't get any worthwhile rest until she pried a few answers out of Trey.

"Th-thanks." Her keys rattled in her trembling hand. She dropped them into her purse.

"Do you want to wait here? I can pick you up."

She shook her head. "I need the walk." Now that she didn't have to hold it together for the patients, her reactions were getting the better of her. She needed to get out of the building quickly.

"That works." He tilted his head toward the door. "Let's roll."

As they moved through the door, the light hit him, and she noticed his puffy cheek. Her jaw sagged. There were two stitches visible at the edge of his hairline. "What happened to you?"

He gave her a gusty sigh. "The blackout didn't work in my favor. Turns out I can't see in the dark without night-vision goggles."

"Are you okay?"

"I'm fine," he said with an exaggerated wink. "The stitches are fake. A sympathy gag."

"Is that so?" She didn't believe him for a minute, but he clearly didn't want to talk about it.

"Is it working?"

"Maybe a little." She smiled up at him. "Did they give you a sticker?" The air outside carried the scent of the harbor. It felt clean and rejuvenating as she breathed in deep. She'd been considering spending her two days off in Asheville for a little holiday snow and cheer. Maybe Trey would go with her. Neutral territory might be exactly what they needed. Leaving him home alone wasn't an option, no matter how much he appeared to have matured.

"I asked for a lollipop." His quick grin flashed and faded. "How bad was it for you?"

"It could've been worse," she admitted. News had traveled quickly through the hospital that two nurses on Franklin's floor were injured by unknown assailants during the blackout. "We didn't have any real problems." She slid into the passenger seat when they reached his car.

"Where are the flowers?" he asked as he started the car.

She closed her eyes and let her head drop back. "I left them on the desk." Though she'd meant to, now it seemed like the weak move. If Trey couldn't deal with David sending her flowers, that was his problem. If this afternoon's outburst was any indication, he'd find something to complain about regardless. "My brain is scattered. I'll go back." She started to open her door, but he stopped her with a light touch on her arm.

"Hang on. I'll send a text and one of the guys at the desk can bring them out."

"Thanks." She wasn't sure what else to say. "You seem to have friends everywhere."

"Is that a problem?"

"Of course not. I'm just admiring the skill."

His text message sent, he backed out of the parking space and shot her a look. "You have friends."

"True." And she wondered if her friend Franklin had followed through on his friendly threat to have a word with David. It felt rude to ask outright and she was more curious about his injuries. "What do you think caused the blackout?"

David shook his head. "I'd hate to guess. I only know about the rogue wall that attacked me."

She appreciated how his humor eased her mind. "All of the walls and corners on our floor behaved," she said as he pulled to a stop at the main entrance. "We had a few tears and upset mamas, but the windows and sunshine worked in our favor."

"That's good." He peered beyond her to the big glass doors. "There you go."

She opened her door and thanked David's

friend for bringing her flowers down. When she was settled, the vase secure between her feet, she turned to him. "Thank you so much. They kept me smiling all day."

"I'm glad." He leaned closer, as though he wanted to kiss her. She wanted that, too. Instead, he patted her hand and put the car in gear. "Have you ever been through a power outage like that before?"

She shook her head, wondering about the status of Franklin's staff. She'd sent him a text message, but he hadn't responded. "Usually the generators kick in right away." To distract herself, she shared the one comical spot in the crisis. "One of the teenagers threatened to sue for breach of trust and mental anguish."

"You're kidding."

Terri laughed softly. "I wish. It was quite a rant. He was gaming when the power died and he said we'd violated the inferred promise of the game as a stress reliever and aid in healing."

"Good grief. Let me guess, only child of trial lawyers."

"No. I think he's a drama major. He's certainly good at improvisation. He made Suzette laugh, and that wasn't an easy task this afternoon."

"Why not?"

Terri sighed. Why hadn't she quit when she

was ahead? "Apparently, Suzette saw Trey before I did this afternoon. She's not his biggest fan."

"That's reasonable."

"It is?"

"Sure," David said, changing lanes to take the exit to their neighborhood. "She's your best friend and from what you said last night, he hasn't been the best of brothers lately."

"This is true." Terri dropped her head back against the seat. "I appreciate her protective streak."

"That's good to hear."

"Why?"

"Because I have one, too," David said.

"That's…" Her voice trailed off as she watched his knuckles go white on the steering wheel. He had strong hands with long fingers and odd tan lines from the gloves he wore for various outdoor sports. She looked closer, noticing the scrapes on his knuckles. It looked like a classic fistfight injury. "Did the wall fight back?"

He shifted in his seat, but there was nowhere for him to hide his banged-up hand. "No, the desk tried to horn in on the action."

"I don't believe you," she blurted, thinking about his knowledge of the police report. "What happened to you in the blackout?"

"Nothing too bad." He shifted again, this time stretching his battered hand on his thigh. "Really," he assured her as he made the turn into their neighborhood. "Do you need a ride to work in the morning?"

"I'm off," she replied. "Though I might need a ride to pick up a rental. I'm not sure how long they'll keep my car."

"Just let me know."

"Thanks." She'd been saying that to him a lot lately. David pulled into her driveway, and she gaped at the big motorcycle parked near the garage. "If he'd been driving that last night, I would've heard him arrive," she muttered.

"Are you saying Trey bought that today?"

"It wouldn't surprise me." From this angle it was impossible to see if there was a license plate on the burly bike. "I never asked how he got to the hospital." She'd been too shocked that he'd shown up. "He told me he has a job and that they were letting him telecommute so he could visit with me. I have no idea about his finances. We haven't discussed any of that yet."

"He dropped out of school for a job?"

She nodded. "He says he met some kind of corporate team during a campus interest fair or something." She didn't want to get into the details of Trey's emotional journey. His explanation didn't sound any better to her now than it had sounded last night. "Maybe he borrowed the bike from a friend."

"You think he stayed in touch with local friends but not with you?"

David's obvious doubt eroded her confidence in the theory, and the implication hurt her already raw feelings. "I guess so. You know how guys are."

"Being one, I have an idea." He cleared his throat. "If he's sugarcoating what happened in Arizona, it's possible he's put you in danger."

"What do you mean?"

David shook his head. "I'm probably just being overprotective. What has he told you?"

"He said college overwhelmed him." She rubbed her forehead. "It's a long story and I was tired. Basically, he got caught up with a group of people who helped him sort things out. There was an emotional and physical boot camp or something. Self-improvement, teamwork and productivity, the whole thing."

"That sounds less like a company and more like a commune or cult."

"You know, I thought the same thing, but it was late. I know there's more to it and he promised to tell me everything."

"Terri." He flexed his hand again, his gaze on the motorcycle. "Cults don't let go of new recruits easily."

Hearing the warning in David's voice, she felt her nerves twisting a little more. "He says he'll tell me all about it," she said. At last she was energized and eager to hear the details.

"Maybe talking it out will clear the air."

He didn't sound the least bit convinced. "It's okay, David. We're a long way from Arizona." She tugged her purse strap through her hands. "Trey can be a jerk, but he wouldn't hurt me. Whether he found himself or only got himself more lost, he'd never hurt me."

"Terri, I don't like this."

Somewhere deep inside, her intuition agreed with him. She picked up the vase of flowers and tried to lighten the mood. "You're just upset we're not going back to Benny's tonight."

"We could." He grinned and reached across to hold her hand. "How about Trey comes with us? I'd like to get to know him."

"Tempting," she admitted. What did it mean that David wanted to know more about her brother? This felt as though it was moving pretty quickly from friends to something more serious. Changing up plans would only give Trey reason to fuss or mope. She'd promised him they'd sort a few things out tonight. "Can I take a rain check?"

David nodded. "Of course."

"Thanks. I want to know what the heck he's been doing since he dropped out."

"Understandable."

David opened the car door, took the flowers from her hands and walked Terri to the porch. She opened her mouth to thank him again, but the words got caught somewhere in the fragrant blooms between them. No hesitation this time. No warning. His lips landed on hers. Gently at first. Setting the flowers on the porch rail, he kissed her again. She kissed him back and his arms came around her, pressing her close to his hard body. Her hands fisted in the fabric of his jacket as she struggled to keep her balance.

He broke the kiss, but his embrace remained strong. "You're rattled and you don't have a car. Invite me in. Let me stay for a bit."

"No." She wanted to say yes and they both knew it. "I'll be fine."

His nostrils flared, and she knew he wanted to argue. "I'm just down the street if you need me."

She smiled up at him, comforted beyond words by his thoughtfulness. His eyes were full of concern, but her lips tingled with the desire sizzling between them. A heady combination. "You're a good friend, David."

"Damned with faint praise," he murmured. His lips brushed against her cheek. "I want more, Terri. Let me take you out for a date that proves my intent."

"Soon, I promise." She felt like a high school

sophomore afraid her dad would catch her making out on the porch. "I'll text you."

He kissed her again. "Tomorrow, then."

"Tomorrow." She smoothed her hands over his shoulders, reluctant to let him go.

He proved himself strong enough for both of them and stepped away. "I'll be waiting for that text."

She grinned, watching him leave and wondering how it was possible to find what might be the right guy at what felt like the wrong time.

"Who was that?"

She jumped at the sound of her brother's voice. He was leaning against the open doorway, studying her with a dark, surly gaze.

Maybe he didn't understand it yet, but she was the one who would be asking the questions.

Chapter Seven

"Flowers for a patient, huh?" Trey's lip curled. "Is the dude why you're so late?" he demanded, jerking his thumb toward the driveway. "Where's your car?"

"It's still at the parking garage." She glared at his back as she followed him inside. Slipping out of her coat, she hooked it on the hall tree and then turned to lock the front door. She didn't understand where all this hostility was coming from. When they were younger he'd get waspish when he was stressed-out, but by his own admission, he'd pulled himself together. Patience was the key, she decided, recalling the counselor's advice. It was possible that even though he said he wanted to be home, it made his survivor guilt worse. Regardless, he was all the family she had left. They'd find a way to talk through his issues.

"There was some trouble at the hospital this afternoon." She carried the flowers to the kitchen and set the vase on the table. "My *friend*," she said, putting a gentle emphasis on the word, "drove me home."

"You couldn't ride with Suzette?"

"Why do you care? Were you wanting to talk with her again?" she countered, pleased when he shook his head quickly. "What's with the Harley out front?"

"I got a bonus," Trey said. "Cade Sutter had an ad on craigslist. Worked out for both of us."

She remembered Cade. He'd been Trey's friend and teammate on the high school baseball team. "Nice." What else could she say? "How'd you earn the bonus?"

"According to the email, I do excellent work." He reached into the refrigerator and pulled out two longneck beer bottles. "Surprised?"

"Of course not." When Trey wanted to succeed, he did. His recovery and determination to go to school out of state proved that.

He popped the top off one bottle and handed it to her. "You look like you could use it."

"No, thanks." She moved past him to clean out her lunch box. "How did you spend your afternoon?"

"Apparently not having as much fun as you," Trey said, slouching into a chair at the kitchen table. "What's his name?"

"David," she said without thinking. "And I wasn't late because of him. Without him I probably wouldn't be home yet." She showed him the picture she'd taken with her phone. "My car was vandalized just before the end of my shift."

"No way." Trey scowled at the damage and sat up straighter. "Who has a problem with you?"

Hope flickered in her heart at his immediate support. This was the brother she knew. "I doubt it was personal. Several cars were damaged and are part of a crime scene until further notice."

"Then I'm glad I bought the bike. I can drive you to work tomorrow."

"I'm off tomorrow," she said. "When did you get your motorcycle license?" she asked, knowing the likely answer was Arizona.

"This afternoon," he replied, surprising her. "I took a class while I was... I got certified. The DMV here validated the class, gave me a road test and I'm good to go."

"Motorcycle certification was part of getting your head on straight?"

"It was a way to pass the time when meditation failed." He softened the defensive retort with a wry smile. "Do we have to talk about it?"

"Yes." She leaned back against the countertop and studied him. "Considering the time and money I invested in your education, I think I deserve the full explanation."

"You want me to pay you back? I can do that."

That wasn't at all what she meant. "Trey, I'm concerned about you, not the money."

"I will. I'd planned to do that anyway," he continued, ignoring her. His beer bottle hit the table with a smack and he pushed to his feet. "Let me get my checkbook."

"Trey, you know—" She trailed after him, that flicker of hope she'd felt moments ago turning to ash.

"*Trey, you know*—that's all I ever hear." He stopped at the stairs and glared at her. "What I know is you'll never let me forget the sacrifices you made."

He might as well have hit her. His brittle words, the old complaints, sapped any lingering sympathy. "Cut the crap." She stalked after him. "What happened to the new, mature you? Forget the damn checkbook. I'm not putting up with one more tantrum. If you've grown up, prove it and *communicate* with me like an adult."

"Just because I found a better solution than a traditional four-year degree—"

"Trey," she warned. "I'm not playing." She took a deep breath. "Mom and Dad raised us better than this. We've had our disagreements and plenty of ups and downs. We always stuck together, right up until you disappeared. I love you. I will always want what's best for you. End of story. If this job is so great, tell me about it. If it's stressing you out now that you're home, tell me about that, too."

She hoped her immense relief wasn't too obvious when he came back down the stairs and flopped down on the couch. The move reminded her of simpler days when the Barnhart family of four would settle in front of the television for movie nights.

"Fine." He took a big breath and let it out slowly. "Rediscover lets me design and create. It started as a kind of occupational therapy, but I guess I was a natural at the programing."

Finally, she had a name to research. "What does Rediscover do?"

"They're big on diversity," Trey said. "The team center is mostly self-sufficient with solar energy and organic gardens. There's only enough for staff and the team, but it's an awesome setup near the dining facility. They have programmers, like me, and all kinds of classes. The more I learned about them, the more they learned about me—it all just fell into place. Everyone works together in areas that interest them."

She couldn't help thinking of communes and cults again, but she kept that opinion to herself. This team had encouraged Trey to come home. She would focus on that. "You'll go back when?" Having him away at school was one thing, but she'd always expected him to settle nearby when he graduated. If not in Charleston, then at least in this part of the country. She wasn't ready to be this alone. David's image immediately came to mind, refuting the idea that she was alone.

"I'm not sure. A month, more or less," he said with a shrug. "While I'm home, can't we keep things the way they were?"

Something in his tone made her edgy. "What do you mean?"

"That David guy. I don't like him."

"You don't even know him."

Trey rolled his eyes. "I don't think it shows much respect for you standing on the porch locking lips like that."

Terri opened her mouth and snapped it shut again, clinging to the fraying edges of her patience. David had been nothing but respectful since the moment they met. Thoughtful, considerate and even protective. "David has been a perfect gentleman."

"Not according to what I saw."

Trey wasn't teasing. She could've handled that. He was baiting her—she could see it on his face. "I don't want to argue. Let's just agree that you don't get a say in how I spend my free time."

"If your brother doesn't watch out for you, who will?"

"I watch out for myself," she said, trying to

keep up. Talking with him was like flipping a coin, and none of it made sense to her. One second the words were kind, and the next they were mean. One minute he wanted to share his experiences, and the next he dismissed her questions. Had this strange team or company he'd found put him on drugs? "What's the real problem?" she blurted.

"Is it so much to ask for some uninterrupted time to reconnect with my sister?"

"Not exactly…" She ran out of words. This was absurd. She'd put her life on hold since the accident and not once had she allowed her grief or career to interfere with her brother's recovery. Franklin had been all too right about that one. She was ready to socialize again, ready to inject some fun into her life. Whether David was Mr. Right Now or Mr. Right, she wasn't going to set a precedent of pushing friends away whenever Trey didn't agree with her choices.

Her heart ached under the weight of her brother's selfishness. He and his team process had let her worry rather than clear up the questions of his safety, and now he wanted to judge and dictate what she should and shouldn't do?

As she'd told him last night, forgiving him for disappearing didn't erase the aftermath. Her love life—though her current situation stretched the definition—wasn't any of his business. Now that a kind, handsome guy was interested, it seemed cruel that Trey would ask her to put that part of her life on hold. Again. "I'm ordering a pizza," she said. It was better than continuing a pointless argument. She pulled out her phone to make the call.

"I could eat," he said. "Don't be mad just because you know I'm right."

She had a mental image of that coin flipping again. "Right about what?" She planted her hands on her hips.

"Watching out for you. I know what I saw," Trey blurted. "You had that dopey look on your face. Like the year you were crushing on the catcher."

She'd been fourteen. "Dopey?" Furious now, she started up the stairs, pizza forgotten. At twenty-six years old with an established career, she didn't have to put up with this. "You are unbelievable." She tried to rein in the explosion simmering under the surface. "This is not the day to mess with me."

"Tell me about him and maybe I can support you."

"Maybe?" She stopped at the top of the stairs, all too eager to throw every example of her excellent judgment back in his face. Closing her eyes, she took a deep breath and counted to ten. Twice. "He's kind. He is new to the hospital and Charleston, but he was raised in Georgia. He comes from a big, close family and he loves the ocean. He has superb manners and he is my friend."

"With benefits," Trey muttered.

That coin flipped again. "That's it," she said. Her temper hit the flash point. She walked into his room and began gathering the few personal items he'd brought home.

"Wait!" he shouted, pounding up the stairs behind her. "What are you doing?"

"Kicking you out."

"You can't."

"Wrong." She closed his laptop and slid it into the protective sleeve. She coiled up the power cord and dropped it into the backpack emblazoned with a Northern Arizona University logo. Seeing that emblem, one that had made her smile with pride in August, only fueled the cold rage inside her now.

She gave him credit for creativity as Trey did his best to break her silence, baiting her with wild accusations about her sex life while she plucked his dirty clothes out of the hamper in the bathroom and tossed those into the backpack, as well.

"This is insane!" he roared. "You're choosing some guy you just met over me?"

She zipped his backpack and shoved it into

his chest. "No. I'm choosing *me* over you. When you can be civil, you're welcome in my home."

"Terri, don't do this."

"Maturity is accepting the consequences, Trey. I love you and wish you well in all of your endeavors."

"I'm sorry," he said, looking truly contrite for the first time in years. "I was rude. Out of line. Please don't kick me out."

She hesitated.

"Dan—"

"David," she corrected.

"David sounds like a winner," Trey said. "I just don't want to see you get hurt."

How ironic that David had made a similar statement about Trey. Maybe she should be the one to leave. She had options, but this was her home. "Why do you assume the worst about me?"

"Not you, him." Trey set the backpack on the floor and pulled her into a big hug. "If he's so great, he'll give us the space we need."

"What about the space you took for yourself without any regard for my feelings?"

"I'm sorry."

She believed him, despite her certainty that the coin would flip again sooner or later. What would he say if she blurted out how much space she wanted from him and his impossible moods?

She sighed. She'd never figure out what had happened if she gave up on him now. "I'm still going out with him if he asks me."

Trey frowned. "God, you're stubborn."

"I get it from my brother."

Regret tugged at his features, making him look older than he was. "I learned from the best," he countered, slinging the backpack over one shoulder.

"Wanting it to be like old times isn't a bad thing," she said quietly. "We just have to honor how we've both changed."

"Fair point," he said. "Can I please stay?"

She shouldn't say yes. "Why don't we order that pizza and put up the Christmas tree tonight?" If they got through that without another fight, she'd consider it. "Then we'll see."

"Cade and I were going to grab a beer—kidding!" She tossed a shoe at him. "Just kidding! Pizza and Christmas sounds good."

With a nod, she went to her room to change clothes. Hopefully, it would be another fresh start. If the memories didn't put them at each other's throats again.

THE MOMENT HE walked in the door, David powered up his secure laptop and checked messages. He didn't like the idea of Terri staying alone with her brother. For the first time since he'd planted the bugs in her house, he cued them up to listen in real time.

Not one of them responded. Great.

He supposed a mass malfunction was possible, but it felt like a stretch. Irritated, he went to the kitchen for a beer. Returning to the den, he debated his options while he wrote up an after-action report on the blackout for the director. He included everything, from Trey's visit to Terri's floor at the hospital to his movements before and during the blackout. Unfortunately, David couldn't prove he'd fought with Trey, though it seemed the most likely explanation.

He hit Send and barely had time for another swallow of beer before his cell phone rang.

"How many men did you see with Trey Barnhart today?" There were no pleasantries when Director Casey called during a case.

"Only one." And he had the stitches to prove it. "I can go back through the—"

"No. I have someone on it."

David was happy for the backup and he waited for further questions or instructions. He'd never heard Casey this agitated.

"They didn't get into Dr. Palmer's ward," Casey said, clearing up David's worst fear. "The patient is fine and the two nurses who were attacked are stable."

David blew out a breath and sent up a prayer of

thanks. He felt guilty that he hadn't been there, even though his job had been to follow Trey. "Aside from Trey and his pal who got me, do you know how many were on the attack crew?"

"Everything we have here says four. It doesn't fit," Casey said. "Everything we know about Rediscover says they strike in teams of five."

"Could the fifth guy have been in the getaway car?"

Casey swore. "So far we haven't located a getaway car on any of the feeds from the video cameras around the hospital."

Not good. Charleston was a great walking city, but the idea of four or five men rushing away from a hospital crisis would be obvious. "Do you have a theory on the vandalism?" David asked.

"Distraction."

That confirmed David's sense of today's events. "You think this was just a test?"

"I'm sure of it. I've spoken to Dr. Palmer already. They didn't get anything. A camera in the corridor shows that one man, not the brother, by the way, entered through the stairwell after the lights went out. He subdued the two nurses stationed outside Dr. Palmer's ward and then made several attempts on the security panel, but didn't break the code."

"Why send in only one guy?" David wondered aloud.

"Has to be a test run," Casey said. "Unless the goal is murder rather than recovery of the biotechnology."

That was a reasonable guess, but both David and the director wanted facts. "Trey cut the power and someone else vandalized the cars," David said. "I saw Barnhart go into the parking garage, but he wasn't there long enough to do that much damage. He doubled back to the hospital to help the guy in the basement."

Casey sighed. "Have you figured out how they recruited him?"

"I have last night's conversation in the archive, but today the bugs are dead."

"That's too coincidental to ignore."

"Agreed. Do you want me to go in with a direct approach?"

"Not yet. If we burn Barnhart we lose our only contact inside Rediscover."

None of this eased his reservations about Trey staying with Terri. "I'll get closer. He picked up a motorcycle at some point today. The picture is in the report. I'll find the pressure point."

"This is a delicate stage for Dr. Palmer's research," Casey said. "If Rediscover blows it, we won't have another chance for five years at best."

"Understood." Though David wasn't technically alone in this, he was coming damn close to overwhelmed. Given another chance at Trey in that dark corridor, he'd be more aggressive.

"I expect Dr. Palmer will call on Terri to fill in for the injured nurses," Casey said. "That may be exactly what Rediscover hoped to accomplish today."

David absorbed that detail. The logic of it chilled him. "Trey's involvement with today's blackout makes it pretty clear they recruited him for her access to Dr. Palmer."

"Speculation doesn't give us enough evidence to round them up just yet."

In the Coast Guard and as a Specialist, David had played with high stakes before but never with an innocent civilian smack in the middle of the game. He had to find a way to get closer to Terri without breaking cover. "Give 'em enough rope to hang themselves, you think?"

"Yes," Casey replied. "I have analysts going over every available camera angle from the hospital's security system and throughout the surrounding area. We'll figure out what they learned today. If Barnhart attempts to use his sister against Dr. Palmer, we need to intervene immediately."

"I'll get it done," David promised. He stared at the phone long after the director had ended the call.

Eventually, he returned to the file on Trey, crossing it with the background they had on Terri, Dr. Palmer and Rediscover. Something in here would show him the next step. It had to. Sure, he could use the personal angle and become the charming new boyfriend, but it would be nice if Terri didn't hate him when this was over.

It wasn't a normal in-and-out covert operation here. When the Rediscover strike team was caught—and he would make sure that happened—David still had to work within his new cover here in Charleston. *For life.*

He laughed at himself. When he'd been presented with this assignment, he thought he'd worked all the scenarios. He hadn't anticipated finding a woman he liked, a woman he'd like to know better. Sure, a long-term relationship would help him adjust here, but he'd be dead in the water if Terri ever found out he'd used her. No woman wanted to learn her trust had been misplaced or abused.

He pushed his hands through his hair and turned his attention back to Trey. What vulnerability had Rediscover exploited? More important, how could David turn that into an advantage? Assuming, of course, that Trey's efforts today hadn't given Rediscover what they needed to steal or destroy Dr. Palmer's research.

David knew he was missing something. They all were. Since they'd met, on the occasions they'd talked about family, Terri described her younger brother as a stable teenager. The accident had changed more than his athletic ability, naturally. But what would make the teenager whose sister had been with him through every step of his recovery turn into a young man who would betray her?

Taking another long pull on the beer, David paced away from the files and the computer. He changed into sweats and hit the treadmill in the home gym he'd set up on the screened porch. Movement helped him think. A pool would be better, but a hard run would suffice. He matched his breath to his stride, letting the case drift through his mind.

Dr. Palmer, a renowned researcher, had been part of Terri's life for a few years. No one kept that a secret. In fact, she'd divided her time since her parents died almost equally between Trey, the doctor and her career. How much time had the doctor spent with Trey?

David's feet kept going, his arms pumping for mile after manufactured mile. His sweatshirt was soaked and he'd drained the bottle of water in the holder when a new theory dawned on him. Trey wasn't about betrayal; he was about salvation. He wanted to shuffle the hand he'd been dealt and come out the hero.

"Damn." David gradually slowed the treadmill to a walk as he tested the idea from all angles. From the brief intel the bugs had gathered last night, Trey had returned with confidence and little regret. When he had visited Terri at work, he'd acted like a young man wanting more than attention; he'd wanted to be noticed. By Terri, sure, but who else had been watching? He considered where and when the team might have been while waiting for the lights to go out.

David went back to his computer and found a message from the Specialist team. The message urged him to review the footage. He opened the link to surveillance footage for the hours before Trey visited Terri's workstation.

The first image was Trey's approach through the front entrance of the hospital. The view widened to the streets around the hospital campus. Four men had approached on foot from the direction of the Market. The men had split up a block away, with Trey heading straight for the main entrance. He was easy to spot in his Arizona sweatshirt. As the footage moved back in time, trolling the street views, David spotted what had prompted the team to send him this video. A fifth man, Joseph Keller, one of Rediscover's shady associates, relaxed at a sidewalk café, soaking up sunshine and coffee.

"Damn." David opened a second window and brought up the file on Joseph Keller to refresh his memory. Ruthless, downright mean, Keller worked only for profit, but he often preached rhetoric of hope and equality. Keller had ties to disgruntled, grassroots independent organizations worldwide. Rediscover was one of several programs planted to gather up lost sheep searching for life's meaning and purpose. Terri had been right to think her brother's account of his time missing sounded like a cult. David's pulse rate started to climb as Director Casey's original scenario took shape. It wasn't just an abstract theory in a file anymore. A woman he cared about was in danger. Trey had been targeted by a known, violent expert. Through Trey, Keller could get to Terri and through her to Dr. Palmer. Dear God.

David resisted the urge to run out of the house and straight to Terri with this news. Trey had joined Keller an hour before the blackout according to the time stamp. Keller didn't make any effort to be discreet as he handed Trey a button camera and a card reader. Dread pooled in David's gut. Assuming that button cam had worked, Joe Keller could very well know David's face after the fight in the basement. The

Specialist-supplied background would hold up under dissection—hell, it was mostly true anyway.

He thought of his family in Georgia, targets now if Keller deemed David a threat to his plan. He thought of Terri. Trey was in her house, the bugs were busted and David was two blocks away. What a mess.

His phone chimed with a text message. He picked it up in a hurry when he saw Terri's number. Had Trey or Keller already taken the next step? He relaxed when he saw the message was her request for a ride to work in the morning. As Casey predicted, Dr. Palmer had asked for her to fill in for the injured nurses on the project. David sent a reply confirming he could give her a lift. If he could get away with spending the night guarding her house, he would.

The attack today might have been a practice run, but David was certain it had also achieved one of Keller's primary goals. All the elements were falling into place now. Through Trey, Keller and his organization now had better access to Palmer's secure wing.

Unable to sit there and wonder, David went for a run through the dark neighborhood. As he passed Terri's house he saw her and Trey setting up the Christmas tree. He hoped like hell she was right to believe Trey wouldn't hurt her. It would be far better if David felt more confident that Trey would only use that card reader and leave before Keller got close enough to hurt her.

But life didn't offer guarantees.

For the sake of his sanity, David jogged up and down the neighborhood, looking for any sign of the strike team. Wishing he could stamp out the threat before Terri was even aware it existed, he was disappointed when he didn't find the bad guys.

He would find them and he would protect her, he promised silently as he passed her house once more.

Chapter Eight

Thursday, December 12, 7:05 a.m.

David left the house early, giving himself time to pick up coffee as a surprise for Terri. He'd planned to do it anyway just to check in. Now, as her designated driver, he had a stronger reason to show up. Since the motorcycle was still there, he ordered three seasonal lattes at the coffee shop drive-through.

"Just being a thoughtful friend," he murmured as he carried the cardboard tray of drinks to Terri's door.

He had his excuses ready for arriving so early, but knowing Terri, it wouldn't be necessary. Both of them preferred to be fifteen minutes early rather than a minute late for anything. He rang the doorbell and found himself hoping Trey wasn't a late sleeper. Knowing he'd likely been identified, David resisted the urge to rattle the guy's cage a little. It would be better for everyone if he could find a positive way to connect with her brother.

When the door opened, it wasn't Terri's pretty green eyes or sweet smile that greeted him. It was her brother's tough glare. David smiled. "Good morning. You must be Terri's brother."

"Who the hell are you?"

"David Martin." He made a small production out of switching hands for a polite handshake.

"Martin?" Trey's grip was hard, his palm dry. "She's never mentioned you." Trey shrugged. "I'll tell her you stopped by."

"No need," David countered, sticking with the nice-guy approach. "I know I'm early. Is that your bike in the driveway?"

"Yeah. How do you know my sister?"

"We work together at the hospital," David said, moving closer to the threshold, forcing the other man back. "We're carpooling today."

"No, you're not. I'll take her in," Trey said, reluctantly stepping back far enough for David to get inside. "Looks like you might have a concussion," he said with a smirk and a nod toward David's forehead as he closed the door.

It was all the confirmation David needed. He'd been identified all right. Irritated that the kid didn't seem to have suffered at all from their scuffle, he thought about giving Trey a preview of what he was really up against. Bad idea.

Trey—and therefore Keller—knew David could handle himself in a close-quarters fight. That particular skill could still be explained by his time with the Coast Guard. What David wanted to do to this guy right now would be tougher to write off as basic self-defense training. He couldn't afford to give Keller another advantage.

David shrugged. "It's cold this morning. I think Terri will prefer my car over the motorcycle."

"You're wrong." Trey shrugged. "You don't know her like I do."

"I know her differently than a brother, that's true," David said calmly.

Trey's reaction as the implication took root was priceless. His eyes hot with anger, he moved a step closer to David. "You son of a—"

"Trey?" Terri stepped into the entry hall, dressed in her scrubs. "Did I hear the—" She stopped short, her hand going to her hair when she spotted her company. "David? Wow, you're early."

"Thought we'd make time for coffee." He held up the tray. "Your brother was just telling me about his bike."

"I was going to make introductions," she said, her face pinched with concern. "After work."

"We managed." David extended the tray of coffees. "The whipped cream is melting."

"Can't have that." She took the tray and headed for the kitchen. "I'm just about ready. Three coffees?"

"You caught me red-handed trying to break the ice." David grinned and turned to Trey. "I took a chance that you drink coffee, too."

"Wrong." Trey glowered at David. "I'll catch up with you later," he said to Terri, clearly irritated. Without a backward glance, he headed upstairs.

"Something I said?" David asked under his breath.

Terri dismissed his concern with a careless wave. "Not at all. He's unhappy because I have to go in today." She looked for the markers on each cup. "Which one is mine?"

"Here." David worked it out of the holder. "Would you rather ride in with him? I'd understand."

"On that beast? In this weather? No way."

David smothered the urge to gloat. This wasn't simply about winning with the woman he wanted to date. The stakes were much higher than that. It was his job to make sure neither she nor the research was destroyed by Trey's misplaced ideals and warped loyalties.

"Thank you," she said after a long sip that left a thin line of whipped cream on her lip. She licked it away and caught him staring. "You have excellent timing."

"I do?"

She nodded, taking another long sip and then setting the cup aside. "I was about to scramble some eggs for a breakfast burrito. Should I make one for you?"

"That would be great."

David took advantage of her distraction as she simultaneously prepped breakfast and packed her lunch bag. He glanced around to be sure Trey wasn't lurking around, then planted a bug near the kitchen table. "I could take you out to lunch in repayment."

"I appreciate the invitation, but I have no idea when I'll have a break."

"Maybe another time." He wouldn't push, not while her brother might overhear them. Coffee in one hand, bugs in his pocket, David walked a few paces away. He'd been in Terri's house a couple of times. The first time was after a hospital staff picnic, when she'd invited him for a beer to unwind. She'd also asked him in when he picked her up on the way to a sea kayak lesson.

Only once had he been through the whole place without her knowledge. It was a good house, well maintained, if a little on the lonely side. If only there was a reason to believe that would change with her brother's arrival. Instead,

David knew the opposite—more heartache—was the most likely outcome. He wished he could warn her or shield her from the worst of Trey's new alliances.

"Nice tree," he said, venturing into the family room that was actually a part of the big open space that included the kitchen. He covertly planted another bug to replace the one no doubt found and disabled by Trey.

Terri's lips curved into a warm smile. "Thanks. Trey and I decided to get in the holiday spirit last night. It went pretty well."

David heard the undertones in her voice. There was more to the story, but she wouldn't tell him now. It could be something as simple as the melancholy of old memories or something as complex as an argument about Trey dropping out of school.

He walked closer to the tree, pretending to admire the ornaments while he looked for opportunity and placement options for the remaining bugs. Noticing a closed laptop on the end table that had to be Trey's, David did one more double check and planted a bug there, too, on his way back to the kitchen.

"Breakfast is ready," she called from the kitchen.

"That was fast," David said, accepting the wrapped burrito she handed him.

"I've got a system," she said.

"I like it." He'd stepped in to brush a quick kiss to her cheek when her brother stomped down the stairs.

She gave Trey a goodbye hug, and David picked up her lunch bag, wondering if she could sense the glare Trey aimed his way. They'd barely cleared the threshold when he heard the dead bolt slam into place behind them. It was all he could do not to laugh.

"I don't think your brother likes me much," he said when they were in his car.

"Trey has his moody moments," she allowed. "I don't think he slept well."

"How come?" He took a bite of breakfast as they waited for the light to change.

She shrugged. "I'm not sure. When I got up this morning I found him asleep on the couch with his computer open. Maybe telecommuting isn't the best option for him."

"He's a big boy. He'll figure it out."

"I hope so." She sipped her coffee. "Thanks for this."

"No problem." Having her along made the short commute downtown more fun. If only he could figure out how to make it more informative. "How was Dr. Palmer doing?"

"He sounded okay. Not great, just okay."

"Should I be worried about you in that ward after yesterday?"

She shook her head. "I'll be fine. Franklin assured me he increased security up there."

"Right."

"Everyone is on alert for anything out of the ordinary now," she said. "If those men tried again, I don't think they'd make it past the lobby."

But Trey was the only one who'd come into the hospital via that route. David cleared his throat, searching for the happy medium between what he wanted to say and what he could say. "Don't forget you can call me if something happens."

He felt her eyes on him and he wondered what she saw.

"Thanks." It was hardly more than a whisper.

"Hey." He glanced at her, saw her trying to hold back some heavy emotion. "What's wrong?"

"It's nice." Her sigh filled the car. "Having someone care."

"I'm glad you like it," he said. "Because I can't imagine not caring about you."

Though he hadn't planned to say anything of the kind, he wouldn't take the words back even if he could. They were true. Before she could respond, he shifted the conversation to safer topics for the rest of the drive, and when he dropped her off at the main lobby doors, her smile was warm and bright once more.

TERRI FELT LIKE a brand-new person as she stepped off the elevator on Franklin's floor. Decorating the tree with Trey last night had been an excellent idea. It had broken the tension and given them something positive to share. Taking a page from David's mother's book, she'd turned on a radio station playing Christmas carols. It was almost impossible to argue with the happy, familiar songs going on in the background. It wasn't perfect, but they were family and it seemed they could agree on that much at least.

Then having David show up with coffee this morning, hearing him all but declare they were in a relationship…that was immensely heartwarming.

She showed her badge to the man standing guard at the doors. The signs of yesterday's attack were everywhere. The wall and desk where the nurses had been attacked were blocked with yellow caution tape, but that did nothing to hide the bullet holes. Terri counted three on the desk alone. To her right, near the doors, the security panel was smashed, the cover dangling open and all surfaces smudged with residue from the crime scene technicians. "Good morning," she said after a moment.

"Morning." He inspected her hospital ID closely.

In a navy polo shirt and khakis, with a menacing-looking gun at his hip, he didn't wear a name tag or uniform like the hospital security team she was familiar with. She couldn't be sure if his presence was new since the blackout. Maybe Franklin had hired private security to protect his patient.

"You can go in," he announced, snapping her back to attention.

"Thanks."

A buzzer sounded as the door beyond the guard opened. Terri flashed him one last smile before hurrying through. She stood in what appeared to be an anteroom. To her left a glass door revealed what looked like an employee break room. In front of her was a closed door. When the door behind her clicked shut, the doors in front of her swung open and she walked into Franklin's ward.

"Wow," she whispered, awestruck. Three patient rooms with views of the harbor were on the far side of the large open space. The ward was laid out much like a typical ICU around what appeared to be a nurses station on steroids. Through the glass panes, she could see all sorts of lab equipment in other areas, and the hum of a nearby MRI machine was unmistakable.

"You must be Terri," a woman with short, dark hair and a bright smile greeted her from the nurses station. "I'm Regina."

"Nice to meet you," Terri replied.

"Thanks for helping us out on your days off. I just can't go 24/7 like I used to."

"You've been here since yesterday?"

"Pretty much. Dr. Palmer called me back right after the blackout. Forgive the extra muscle out there. Everyone is edgy."

"Understandably," Terri said.

"Dr. Palmer will speak with you soon, but I can show you the setup." Regina smiled. "He said you were a friend of his?"

"Yes, but I don't know a thing about the project."

"Well, that's no surprise. Dr. Palmer doesn't divulge much."

A door slammed, making both women jump. Regina leaned in. "Boss's office," she explained. "He's had people stopping in for meetings constantly. As I said, everyone is edgy after yesterday. Follow me."

Regina's thorough tour took longer than Terri had anticipated. She'd known Franklin couldn't possibly be working in an ordinary ward, but the scope of his resources surprised her.

"Last stop," Regina said, heading back to the anteroom between the ward entrance and the secure door. "Our break room." Terri followed her in. A table for four was positioned near the glass wall that overlooked the ward. The opposite corner was a kitchenette with a microwave and refrigerator. "Lockers, full bathroom and sleeping area are through that door. After yesterday all personal belongings and cell phones have to stay in the lockers now."

"No problem," Terri said. She took the first open locker and stowed her purse, leaving her lunch in the refrigerator.

"Our patient is a nice guy," Regina said as they returned to the ward. "We have a few minutes before the next vitals check. I'll introduce you then."

"Sounds good." Terri tucked her hands into her pockets, wondering what to do next. "What's protocol for the patient if we have another power outage?"

"The patient isn't on any equipment. He was pretty calm yesterday." Regina sighed. "I think that's what this morning's big meeting is about. Dr. Palmer wants his own generator for this ward."

Terri didn't know who bankrolled his research or what he was developing this time, but she knew he had plenty of influence.

"He'll get it," Regina said. "I know I'm just support staff, but it's a nice perk to not have to inventory every alcohol swab."

Raised voices carried through Franklin's closed office door, but it was impossible to make out the words. Terri was relieved when a quiet alarm went off and Regina stood up. "Let's introduce you to the patient. I think you'll get along great."

Regina knocked on the door as she opened it, and Terri heard the soft murmur of a television as they walked in.

"Matt?" she called. "Are you awake?"

"Always."

Regina pulled back the thin privacy curtain and made introductions. "Terri will be part of the team for a while."

"Great to meet you," Matt said, not quite meeting her gaze. "Welcome to the sci-fi ward."

"Thanks," Terri replied with a smile as she adjusted the stethoscope to take his blood pressure and check his pulse. Regina asked Matt several questions and tested his eyesight while Terri watched.

Back at the nurses station, Regina explained the questions. "Matt has an implant in his eye. It's our job to make sure it isn't impeding his vision or causing him discomfort. Tomorrow Dr. Palmer will implement the next stage, which will allow him to monitor the implant performance on a long-term basis."

Terri knew other medical implants had similar capability. She was curious about Franklin's goal with the research, but she knew better than to ask. If she needed to know, Franklin would tell her.

Regina finished adding the vitals to Matt's chart and closed the file. "We don't have anything going on for a bit." She handed Terri a thin folder. "Would you mind getting familiar with Matt's schedule while I catch a nap?"

"Not at all." Terri had the schedule memorized within a few minutes and wasn't quite sure what to do with the time. If she stayed on the project, she'd be sure to bring in a book for her next shift.

A few minutes later, Franklin emerged from the office and escorted a man in a suit out of the ward. When he returned, alone, he aimed a weary smile at Terri. "I'm glad you're here," he said. "Have you met Matt?"

"Regina introduced us."

"Good," he said, his smile faltering. "You'll need to keep an eye on him when he goes to the gym in about an hour."

"Right." She motioned to the folder. The cautions relating to every activity had been spelled out. "Blood pressure and heart rate are still prime concerns?"

He beamed at her. "I should've brought you in at the beginning. I just didn't..." His voice trailed off and his gaze drifted toward the patient's room. "High blood pressure was a problem early on. This interface is a big improvement." He started to say more and then changed his mind. "You can read up on our progress if you'd like." He came around the desk and opened a file for her. "I'll be in my office if you need anything."

Curious, she read through the material, astounded by Franklin's research. Matt had suffered a mild injury to his eye, and this implant, when fully functional, would gather, store and transmit anything and everything Matt observed. The first transmitter test was scheduled for tomorrow. It wasn't a particular cure for blindness; in fact, the practical uses and implications weren't clear to her, but she understood enough to know that if successful this would change biomechanics and nano medicine around the world. No wonder they were taking so many security precautions.

And it explained yesterday's strange attack on Franklin's ward. Someone wanted to impede or even steal his work. She was suddenly grateful for the man with the gun guarding the entrance.

The doors parted with a loud whoosh, and Terri popped to her feet as the man in the suit stormed inside. He glared at her, his nostrils flaring, and went straight for Franklin's office.

She was surprised he left the door open. "That woman needs to go," he shouted at Franklin.

Terri ducked her head, trying desperately to disappear.

"Close the door, Wallace," Franklin said.

"No. I don't care if she can hear me. Bring her in and ask her what she knows."

Terri kept her head down, hoping it was just a matter of a new face in an established project, but really, what else was Franklin supposed to do with two of his nurses out of commission?

"I'll do no such thing."

"Her brother." Wallace lowered his voice so Terri couldn't hear.

Her nerves jangled. What could a total stranger know about Trey? She shouldn't be listening. It wasn't her business and her brother had rarely interacted with Franklin. She thought about stuffing gauze in her ears, since she couldn't leave her station or close the door without being noticed.

Wallace's voice rose once more. "You are deliberately sabotaging your best work. I want to know why."

"You're overreacting. You, of all people, know what this project means to me. Her brother is irrelevant."

A chime sounded on the station monitor, signaling that Matt needed her. She practically raced to his room. "Is everything okay in here?"

He was in the recliner watching television. "Figured you could use the distraction. Wallace is a blowhard. Don't worry about it."

"Thanks," she said. "Do people show up and argue with Franklin often?"

"More than they should. Usually it's about funding."

The current argument sounded far more specific than the request for the generator Regina had mentioned.

"Relax. Franklin trusts you."

"How do you know?"

Matt looked at her, his dark gaze assessing. Then he shrugged. "If he didn't, you wouldn't be here."

Watching the game show network with Matt, she waited out the confrontation. When she saw Franklin ushering Wallace out of the ward, she was ready to return to her station. Before she could put thought into action, Franklin walked into the room. "Matt, if your workout could wait a few minutes, I need a word with Terri."

Matt acquiesced with a nod, and Terri followed Franklin to his office.

"You couldn't have missed that," Franklin began.

"No," she admitted. "Why would anyone around here care about my brother?"

Franklin settled into his chair with a heavy

sigh. "You're aware I've worked on many sensitive projects. As a longstanding friend and an occasional employee, you've been vetted by certain agencies and organizations as part and parcel of my background."

It made sense, but it didn't explain the worry over Trey.

"Your brother was missing," he said. "Dropped out of college early in the semester and you didn't tell me."

She nodded. Ashamed now that she hadn't confided in him. "I'm sorry if that caused you problems. Trey's actions were embarrassing and I didn't want to share that humiliation."

Franklin waved off her response. "It's water under the bridge now that he's home again. Wallace is concerned, from a security point of view, since no one knows why Trey disappeared or where he went. Everyone gets nervous as a project nears live testing and completion. People who don't know you think that your brother, coming home at this critical juncture, makes you a risk to the program."

"You can trust me," she vowed.

"Exactly what I told Wallace."

"Trey and I never talk about my work. His only concern with my job is when I'll be home."

Franklin acknowledged that with a nod. "You'll tell me if he gets curious now?"

"Of course."

"Did he tell you anything about where he went after dropping out?"

"It sounds like he got involved with a self-help group near Sedona."

"Plenty of those out there." He tapped his pen against the desk blotter. "Wallace said he was in the hospital just before the blackout yesterday."

The implication startled her. "He came by the nurses station and asked me to lunch," she said. "He was irritated when I couldn't make time for him, but he left. That was at least half an hour before the problems began."

"I see."

She got the distinct impression Franklin understood more than she did. About all of this. "I promise I won't let you down."

"If I thought otherwise I would have called someone else to fill in."

She relaxed, smiling as his words so closely echoed those of his patient.

"What is it?" he asked.

She met his gaze. "Matt just told me the same thing."

Franklin smiled, looking like a proud father. For some reason that made her want to hug him, but this didn't seem like the right place. After he'd gone to bat for her, she didn't want the security team thinking his support of her was based on sentimental factors. "I'll just, ah, get Matt to his workout."

"Thank you, Terri."

She walked away, perplexed by the number of people who didn't trust her brother. If this commune or team or company from Sedona was so terrible, why hadn't the PI she'd hired figured that out?

Trey wasn't faultless, and his quick-change attitude bothered her, but she couldn't see him going from lost college guy to security risk on a medical research project. It just didn't fit. He didn't care much about medicine or health care, having had his fill of doctors, exams and operating rooms after the accident.

The choices he'd made in Arizona didn't change her love for him. He was family, all she had, and he was home. For now. If by some strange twist Trey had brought trouble to her door, she wouldn't allow him to interfere with Franklin's research.

Chapter Nine

Getting Terri to work on time meant David was at his desk earlier than his coworkers. He made the most of the extra time, first reading through the reports filed by the security team and then taking an investigative walk through the parking garage.

Director Casey handpicked all Specialists who became a part of Mission Recovery. David, like the others, was the best at unraveling an enemy's intention. As the Specialist on site, with the benefit of full access to every element within the hospital, including all security levels, David felt the pressure to figure this mess out. *Quickly.* At the very least it was up to him to provide Casey with a clearer image of the big picture.

Whether it was a distraction or not, with Keller in town, David knew there was a purpose behind the vandalism in the parking garage. The man just didn't do things for the fun of it.

The cars had been processed, but the crime

scene tape was still up. The owners, Terri included, would probably be able to reclaim their cars later today. According to the security footage, Trey had moved through the parking level below and then circled back to the hospital, away from the main lobby elevators. He'd never been close to the vandalized area.

David kept asking himself what Keller's men had learned during the blackout. The logical reason for any test run was to assess reactions and previously undetected threats. Keller now knew response times for Dr. Palmer's ward and the maintenance crew. But what was special about this parking level? It had taken several minutes for the security guard downstairs to get up here and chase off the vandal. If not for the alarm on one of the cars, the vandalism might have gone completely unnoticed until one of the car owners got off shift and reported the problem.

He mentally ticked through the names of the owners whose cars had been damaged. He was biased, of course, concerned that threatening Terri had been the real goal.

David forced himself to evaluate what would have happened if the car alarm hadn't gone off. He studied the damage. Scraped paint, dented fenders and cracked bumpers were the most obvious. Two windows were broken, one passenger side and the driver's side window on the sedan right next to it. Only Terri's car had slashed tires.

David knew the guard on duty most days listened to hard rock music while he did homework for his college courses. He relied on the vibration setting on his phone, along with the lights displayed on the control panel and his radio to keep up with the less-than-demanding tasks of babysitting the parking garage. The music would've blocked out the noise of the vandalism.

David planted his hands on his hips. Only employees parked on this level. Parking here would draw too much attention and put too many factors out of the strike team's control. Employee parking cards had to be scanned going and coming from the garage.

The vandal wanted the access cards. Pulling up the report on his phone, he scrolled through, looking for any mention of items stolen from the vehicles. Not one owner, not even Terri reported a missing access card.

Still, he wasn't ready to ditch his new theory. David ducked under the crime scene tape and peered into each car. Two of the three drivers kept their cards visible. Maybe Keller hadn't wanted to steal the cards, but merely copy one.

David pulled out his phone and called his boss. Casey listened as he explained what he'd found and his new suspicions. "Keller gave Trey a card reader, so it stands to reason he had another for the vandal."

"Keep going," Casey said.

"I'm away from my desk, but I think it's a safe bet if we check the activity in the handicapped spaces, we'll find the wheelman. That's how they left the hospital unseen."

"What do you mean?"

"The vandalism was a distraction," David continued. "They get the cards to copy for the real attack, and when the guard is upstairs chasing off the vandal, the shack is empty and they can drive off as if nothing happened."

"I'll have our resources here look for it," Casey said thoughtfully. "The man who tried to breach Dr. Palmer's ward used something that drained the battery backup on the security panel."

"They thought a dead battery would let them bust through the door?"

"Apparently. I hadn't expected that," he admitted. "It's an old-school approach."

Surprising the director wasn't common. Unfortunately for Keller, David knew doing the unexpected would only make Casey and the Specialists work harder to stop him.

"One more thing," David said, staring at Terri's flat tires. He hesitated. Maybe he was being too protective, too paranoid. "Terri Barnhart's car is the only one that couldn't have been driven away. Do you think it's possible they wanted to send a message to keep Trey motivated?"

Casey's low whistle was confirmation enough that David wasn't far off the mark.

"Terri could be used against Trey or Dr. Palmer," Casey agreed. "Stay close to her. Dr. Palmer plans to stay at the hospital with his patient. I'll send in backup to cover Trey and Keller."

"Yes, sir." He wasn't going to argue over the need for reinforcements. It was a relief he wouldn't have to divert his attention from Terri. Still, with Keller in the area, David thought it would be smart to get some sort of tracker on the doctor as a precaution.

Heading back to work, he followed Trey's path into the hospital and down to the morgue level. He wanted to check out the maintenance area. What he wouldn't give for a few minutes alone with Trey in a small room and no witnesses. What could the kid be thinking to put his sister at risk and then act as if David was the problem? Hard as he tried to put himself in Trey's shoes, David couldn't imagine anything that would make him deliberately put his sisters in harm's way.

When the service elevator stopped on the basement level, David stepped out into the corridor and turned toward the service area, hearing voices as he approached. The electrical crews were still assessing the damage and upgrading security protocols. He made a note of the contractors involved as he walked by. From the look of things, they wouldn't be done anytime soon, a fact that he hoped meant a breather for Dr. Palmer's project. If cutting the hospital's power remained an essential element to Keller's plan, he couldn't repeat yesterday's effort without a crowd of witnesses.

As David climbed the stairs to the HR offices, he wondered again what Keller had learned from yesterday's exercise. One thing was glaringly clear—Keller and his crew were more than willing to cause physical harm to anyone who got in their way.

David wasn't afraid of a fight, and with every passing hour he was more determined to make sure Joseph Keller had hurt his last innocent person.

AT PRECISELY FOUR O'CLOCK, Terri walked into Matt's room, taking care of the last monitoring before she turned his care back to Regina for the night.

"Forgive me, but I forgot your name."

"Terri," she replied, not offended in the least.

"You remind me of my wife, Terri."

She wasn't sure how to respond. His eyes drifted to the window, and his smile was tinged with sadness.

"She never forgot a face or a name and I relied on her for that."

Hearing him refer to her in the past tense, Terri wanted to offer some comfort. Matt didn't seem old enough to carry this much pain. "How long were you together?"

"Not long enough. Can I get up?"

"Go right ahead. I'm done." She watched him walk to the window, uncertain if she should stay or go.

"She died on our honeymoon," Matt blurted. "Franklin may not have told you."

"He didn't. All I know about the project is what I've heard today."

"You probably think I'm an idiot for being the guinea pig."

"Not with Franklin as your doctor."

Matt acknowledged that with an arching eyebrow and a tight smile. "Good point. I volunteered," he said.

For several minutes they watched the afternoon sunlight glint off the dark water of the harbor. She couldn't help remembering that lovely walk she and David had taken along the seawall—before the latest insanity with Trey had started. "Are you having second thoughts?" she asked, determined to focus on her patient.

Matt shook his head. "Never. Whether it fails or succeeds—and everything points to success—it will be worth it."

"A good attitude is more than half the battle."

"You don't know."

Once more she found herself waiting for an explanation.

"I'm Franklin's son-in-law. If being married for less than a week counts for anything."

"It counts," she said quickly, her mind reeling with that announcement. Matt had married Franklin's only daughter? She couldn't recall ever seeing a single photo of the wedding in Franklin's home.

"We were honeymooning in Vancouver," he said, his voice barely a whisper. "She'd never been to the area and we had a grand tour planned."

Terri waited, her breath stalled out in her lungs. The agony was stamped into every nuance of his face, and his shoulders were hunched against a persistent, invisible pain.

"It was a trolley," he rasped. He twisted around in an explosion of movement that sent his dinner tray table rolling into the opposite wall. "What kind of sick mind conspires to blow up a trolley?"

The rhetorical question reverberated in the room as Matt's chest heaved with his ragged respiration. She wanted to tell him to calm down, but she couldn't say the words. She knew from experience that the anger wouldn't stay bottled up, and he needed to give it an outlet.

"The footage they show on television during a tragedy is nothing like being in it. The chaos. The noise." He inhaled. "The silence is worse." He looked up, but Terri knew he didn't see her at all. "One minute we were holding hands with everything to live for. In the blink of an eye, she was dying in my arms on the street of a beautiful city."

Terri kept her thoughts to herself, though she was praying desperately for Matt, for any words that would help him.

"She said she loved me. In that last moment, she said she loved me. She smiled." He turned away, pressing his forehead to the window glass. "Some nut-job group spouting a message about equality killed my wife and ten others, including two children, and injured countless more that day. They planned and prepared and they got away." He moved from the window to the edge of the bed. "What the hell is equal about that? They got away. The people who planted that bomb, who killed *eleven* people, lived," he finished, his voice raw.

Terri had known grief and pain, had felt robbed when her parents died so unexpectedly and far too early. She hadn't known anything like this. Grief wasn't a contest, but Matt's anguish put her situation into perspective. Her world had been tossed on its ear four years ago, but the accident had been random. She couldn't fathom the horror of knowing someone deliberately struck out, killing for the sake of harvesting fear and gaining a headline.

"I'm sorry," she whispered.

"They got away, but I volunteered. I wanted to be part of the solution."

The goal of Franklin's new research became clearer to Terri. An embedded device that could transmit real-time observations and data would tip the scales in favor of the good guys. "You're a hero."

Matt's laughter was low and bitter. "You never met her, Franklin's daughter, did you?"

Terri shook her head. "I only met Franklin four years ago." He must have been working on this project even then.

"She was amazing. Smart like her father, but far more beautiful. A compassionate heart."

Terri smiled at his joke, pleased that he seemed to be calming down.

"I could hardly believe my luck that she noticed me. Fell in love with me. That she said yes when I proposed."

"My dad used to say the same about my mom." Terri had let herself forget what devotion and commitment, what a love so deep and true looked like.

"I've had therapists tell me I'm exaggerating the emotion because of the grief, but she was my whole world."

"That's beautiful," Terri assured him. "It's how love should be. Strong, intense and—"

"Peaceful," he finished for her. "Don't get me wrong, we weren't picture-perfect. Just perfect for each other."

"Exactly," she agreed, moving to clean up the mess in the corner. He didn't need the distraction of a janitor right now.

"I'll do that," Matt said, kneeling beside her to gather up the pieces of broken dishes. "Sometimes I hate the normal stuff."

She sat back on her heels and smiled at him. "I understand. It gets under your skin and makes you itch until the tantrum hits and you have to do *something*."

He stared at her. "You do understand."

She nodded. "I broke more than my share of normal things after my parents died."

"Thanks for not judging."

"No problem." With the mess squared away, she stood. "You're a doing a remarkable and courageous thing here," she said, picking up his chart on her way to the door.

"You think I'm doing this for good and noble reasons."

She paused. "You're subjecting your body to experimental devices, trying to make something good out of an inexplicable act of terror."

"You're wrong. It sounds altruistic your way. Honestly, I'm not here to help others," he said, returning to his chair. "I'm in it for revenge. Franklin has the funding and knowledge to make a difference and empower the good guys in a variety of ways. Me?" He rolled his shoulders. "I'm just a guy who had to sit back and deal with it. There wasn't a place for me to get involved, not a place that would have any impact on the group who tore my life apart. Until now. Franklin can implant anything," he said in a voice so calm it scared Terri. "He can test on me all he wants if it means someone will have the tools to wipe out the team who killed my wife."

The statement left Terri speechless.

"I tried," he said, his eyes earnest. "I threw myself into the causes she believed in. It helped, but that feeling faded too quickly. I pitched in to build better communities, but I couldn't shake the image of some other guy's wife bleeding out after the next attack. What Franklin wants to do is drastic, but it matters. I loved her, Terri, and the men who stole her from me don't deserve to keep walking away."

She mumbled something she hoped he interpreted as encouragement and returned to the nurses station.

Intense didn't come close to what she felt now. It would take some time for her to figure it out. As she left the ward for the day, she couldn't decide which part troubled her most about what had to be the strangest shift of her career.

Franklin had requested her because he knew her personally. He fought for her to stay despite her brother being viewed as a potential security risk. Franklin's project, the full scope of it, swirled around in her brain.

And Matt. What did it mean to love someone so much you'd subject your body to whatever was necessary to empower a fight you'd never see?

She stepped off the elevator at the main lobby and checked her cell phone as she approached the security desk. She was about to ask for a cab when she saw the message that Suzette's brother was taking care of immediate repairs to her car.

DAVID PAUSED JUST out of Terri's line of sight, simply enjoying the view. With her gentle accent, her long, glossy hair and her wide, gracious smile, she epitomized the beauty and charm that set Southern women apart. It sounded ridiculous even in his head and he could practically hear his sisters cackling over the news that, as much as he traveled, he preferred Southern women.

Veering sharply from that line of thought, he noticed the signs of fatigue on Terri's face. He hadn't heard of any trouble upstairs, but it looked as though her shift for Dr. Palmer had worn her out. He wanted to suggest she take time off or ask her about the project so she could share what must be a burden. Neither was a valid option. She couldn't tell him anything about the research and he couldn't tell her his real purpose here. In all probability he knew more than she did about the endgame of Dr. Palmer's work.

"Hey, Terri," he said, striding up to the desk. "Do you need a ride home?"

She turned and her lips curved into a smile, bringing a light into her soft green eyes. "No, I'm waiting on the repair truck." She held up her phone. "Suzette sent her brother to deal with the tires and he's working up an estimate on the body work. Then he'll bring it to me here."

"Great. I'll wait with you."

Her smile, while content, was a little tired at

the edges. "You have better things to do than wait with me."

He shook his head. "I can't think of a single one."

"Stop it," she said, moving toward the seating area in the lobby. "I don't want you to get into trouble."

"Let's see. Human Resources is my job. You're human and a valuable resource. Ergo, I'll stay until your car arrives."

She arched one golden brown eyebrow. "Ergo?"

"Are you a therefore girl?" The joke earned a chuckle out of her. "Seriously, how was your shift?"

"Fine."

He bumped her shoulder with his. "Not so convincing."

"It was good. I mean it," she added when he gave her another bump. "It was exhausting, though. I'd talk about it if I could."

He could see the truth of that in her eyes. "The project isn't why I'm sitting here." It was only a small fib. "You are."

"David," she said on a soft sigh. "Thanks for that."

They sat for several minutes in the quiet, watching people come and go. "You look like you could use a hug."

"If you hug me right now, I'm likely to cry."

"That bad, huh?"

She sighed. "More like that good." She shifted in the seat, facing him and propping her elbow on the back of the chair. "You know Dr. Palmer and I go way back?"

He nodded.

"And you've been here long enough to know there are days that patients teach us more than any formal education."

"Right. Was today a school of hard knocks day?"

"Emotionally," she admitted. "Dr. Palmer has known this patient a long time."

David hung on every word, hoping like hell they didn't have a security problem inside Dr. Palmer's team.

"He's a great guy. A widower," she added. "He told me about his wife today. How they met." Terri sucked in a shaky breath. "How she died."

David reached out and swiped the tear from her cheek before she could.

"I can't get into a ton of detail, obviously, but his story moved me. The way he loved her. Loves her," she corrected herself with a quick shake of her head. "That devotion." She swallowed. "It's intense. I…"

"Go on," he urged, wanting to hear what part of the story had made such an impact.

"She was killed on their honeymoon." She tipped her head to the ceiling. "Can you imagine having your soul mate torn away like that? Before you had any time at all?"

He thought of his sisters, all happily married, and his parents, closing in on their fiftieth anniversary.

"I just… After Mom and Dad died…" She cleared her throat and tried again. "I know it sounds silly, but I think I forgot what that kind of love looks like. My parents were close and affectionate and fun."

"So are mine."

"Then you know what I mean." Her green eyes were hopeful despite the sheen of tears. "I must sound like a dork."

"No way."

Her lips curved into a wobbly grin. "It's terribly sad and still so beautiful. The choices he's made to honor his late wife. To defend her memory. Not his words," she said, "but his intention. In my opinion."

Her opinion was suddenly the only one that mattered to David. He wanted to touch Terri's hair, her skin, to give her that sense of connection she so obviously craved. He wanted to give her every good thing she deserved. Not to fulfill orders or for the advancement of the case, but for himself. The awareness startled him.

"It's been years since I let myself think about anything more than the next therapy session, the next shift or paycheck," she went on.

"You've had more than your fair share of stress recently." And she'd have more to come if Trey was in as deep with Keller as it appeared.

Her chin bobbed as she nodded. "Just when it started to ease up, Trey went missing."

"But he's back now," David soothed. "You can relax." He couldn't tell her he'd take the lead on managing her stress. "Let me take you out tonight. We'll do something special."

"Thanks, but I'll be okay."

"You're already more than okay." When she met his gaze, he gave her a wink. "A day like this calls for a night out."

"I don't know." Her phone caught her attention. "Oh. My car's done."

"Good." He wasn't taking no for an answer. "You can unwind a bit and I'll take care of everything. Come on, we'll have fun, I promise."

"You don't have other plans?"

"No." His only plans would've involved staking out her house. Better to spend that time with her rather than watching over her. He walked her out to her car when it arrived and held the driver's door open for her. "I'll pick you up by seven," he said after she'd finished her business with Suzette's brother. "We'll get dressed up and celebrate."

Her eyebrows rose. "Celebrate what?"

"It's Thursday and the weather's clear," he said. "Those are good enough reasons for me." Keeping a beautiful woman safe, checking for any dangers lurking in her home—that was just an opportunity to multitask.

"It's a generous offer, David, but I can't keep relying on you to cheer me up when I'm down."

"Of course you can."

She tilted her head, studying him. "You aren't going to drop this, are you?"

He leaned in close, watched her eyes go wide and then kissed her. Softly and not too quickly. In front of the hospital where they both worked. They both knew what kind of statement he'd just made. "Not a chance."

She was still blinking owlishly when he closed the door for her. He figured most of the nursing staff would have heard about the kiss before he returned to his desk.

Oddly enough, mission or not, he discovered the idea of rumors circulating about him and Terri didn't bother him in the least.

Now all he had to do was come up with a plan for a stellar evening. Confirming the clear skies and balmy weather would continue, he started making calls. He did a quick search of mansion tours, carriage rides and restaurant specials. While those options held some appeal, she'd been born and raised here and seen it all with holiday decorations and without.

This had to be different. Something special just for her. He wanted to give her an experience she'd never had, one that would leave her with fond memories, in case his assignment destroyed their friendship.

After everything she'd told him, the least he could do was show her what an amazing woman he saw when he looked at her. Pulling up the tide charts, he set to work out the details. He would give her an evening she couldn't dismiss later as a tactic or trick, no matter how the case with her brother ended.

Chapter Ten

David arrived at Terri's house just before seven o'clock and noticed Trey's motorcycle was gone. He wasn't sure if that should be a relief or cause for worry, based on Keller's presence in the area.

He'd accept it as good news for the moment, knowing it would be better for Terri if she didn't have to watch another awkward conflict between brother and boyfriend.

Boyfriend. The word echoed in his head. He buttoned his suit coat as he walked to the door, waiting for the expected jolt of shock over the concept. It didn't happen. As he pressed the doorbell, he realized he was okay with the idea.

Not because it was an undercover role, but because he liked Terri. She was definitely as pretty as the dates his sisters had sent him on. Prettier. But she appealed to him on a deeper level. Her sense of humor, her energy and her loyalty all made the outside appearance lovelier.

She opened the door and his thought process

stalled. She looked… "You…" His voice, the traitor, failed him.

He vaguely recalled his sisters and mother rambling now and then about the perfection of a little black dress. Terri had elevated the term to an art form. Cut low in front, the dress wrapped around her curves, nipped in at her narrow waist and flared out again, the fabric swirling softly just above her knees.

"Wow," he said, trying again.

"Is it too much?" She did a quick, full turn. "You said dress up and… Why are you staring?"

He caught her hands and tugged her close, silencing her with a soft kiss. "You look stunning," he said. "Better than stunning." He liked the happy glow in her eyes.

"What's better than stunning?"

"You." He hadn't realized he needed this respite as much as she did. Knowing what was in store, eager to see her reactions, he was going to enjoy every minute of the evening ahead.

"You don't look so bad yourself," she said, her gaze cruising over him. "This is a good look on you."

"Thanks." Suddenly all the intel he'd reviewed today crashed in on him. As they had peeled back the layers on Keller's connections and operations, it seemed the threats went deeper, winding into areas that made Casey nervous. The facts were bad enough, but the potential for numerous disasters right here in Charleston? That had David wound too tight.

With an effort, he pushed those thoughts of danger and risk out of his mind, focusing on Terri. Tonight was for her. "Right this way," he said, offering his arm after she'd locked the door.

"How gallant," she said with a little laugh. "Can I ask where we're going?"

He liked the way her hand curled around his arm. "You can ask." Her fragrance wafted around him, and he thought he could be content right here. "It doesn't mean I'll answer."

"Hmm, mysterious." Her smile made him feel as if he'd won the lottery. "I'll wait and be surprised."

He hoped she would be. Pleasantly. He opened the car door for her, appreciating the view of her toned legs as she sank into the seat. He'd pulled things together pretty quickly, but he thought he nailed it. They'd know soon enough. She was quiet on the drive out to the marina where he kept his boat docked. "Still thinking about the patient?"

"No. I left work at work. Thanks to you."

"What did I do?"

"You listened," she said. "And then you kissed me in front of everyone."

"Everyone?" He snorted. "Hardly. A few strangers and one guy on the valet team—"

"Suzette's brother saw us."

He slid a glance her way, caught her smiling. "So that's how word got around before I got back to my desk."

"Seriously?" There was a note of delight in her voice.

"Pretty much," he said. "Did it bother you?"

"That depends," she said. "Why'd you do it?"

"Isn't it obvious?" He reached out and caught her hand. "I like you." He wished it would stay that simple. "I like kissing you."

"Sound reasoning," she said after a minute.

"Were you expecting another one?" He caught the movement as she shook her head. Then it hit him. "Your brother said something."

"Not about the kiss at the hospital," she clarified. "He wanted to hang out tonight, but I told him we had plans."

David felt a rush of gratitude for Dr. Palmer's patient who'd put her in that strange bittersweet mood that inspired her to take him up on his offer to go out tonight. He should probably say something about not wanting to interfere with her relationship with her brother, but they hadn't exactly hit it off and she'd know he was lying. Whether or not she called him on it, it would make her question other things about him, and that wasn't a risk he could take.

"You don't like my brother much," she said as he parked at the marina.

Maybe they were on the same wavelength. He cut the engine and swiveled in the seat, earning her full attention. "I've been your friend only for a few weeks, so I don't have much right to say anything."

"But you want to."

"Oh, yeah." He sucked in a breath. "It'll wait for another night. Let's keep tonight about you. *Us*," he added, emphasizing the word, hoping she'd agree.

"Just as soon as we step out of this car, it will be. Right now just say it," she said. "I don't want it hanging over me like a storm cloud tonight."

"Terri—"

"Come on, it can't be any worse than what I think you want to say."

He immediately dialed back the rant. "No one's perfect and I understand as well as anyone what it's like to be a little brother. My sisters don't take enough credit for teaching me how to fight dirty."

"Disclaimer noted." A smile tugged at the corner of her lips. "Go on."

He wanted to kiss her, right there. If he gave in to that urge, they wouldn't make it to the boat.

"I don't like the way he treats you. You give and give, and from where I'm standing he takes it all for granted. Not just the money you worked so hard to earn to get him into school, but the effort and love, too. You deserve better."

She nodded, her eyes sad.

He could spit nails for letting Trey horn in on this evening. "Look, I should say something noble about family ties and give you a rain check on our date." He tipped up her chin so he could look into her eyes. "I can't give you the words, but I will drive you back home if that's what you want."

"I'd rather be with you."

Why did that simple declaration make him feel as if he'd found a shipwreck filled with treasure? "Good." He hurried out of the car and came around to open her door. Her smile was almost back to full power.

He kept her hand in his as he escorted her out to his boat. "Careful of your heels," he said, glancing at the sexy, strappy sandals. They gave her enough of a boost that her lush lips were within easy reach. As if to prove it to himself, he stopped short and pulled her close, his hands resting lightly at her waist when his lips found hers. "I'm glad," he said, leaning back, "you're here with me."

She licked her lips. "Me, too."

He stepped into the boat first, then helped her aboard and kissed her again.

Her smile was priceless, dreamy as her fingers traced the lapels of his sport coat. "Do you greet all your passengers this way?"

"Not a chance. This is my first date on my boat."

"You're joking."

He gave her a wounded expression. "I am not. Until now, I might as well have put up a No Girls Allowed sign." He laced his fingers with hers and led her to the wheelhouse. "Come on."

He couldn't wait to see the look on her face when he started the engine.

Holding her hand, he turned the key, ridiculously proud of himself when her eyes went wide and she clapped her hands over her mouth.

Yeah, he'd nailed it. He led her around the console and onto the bow. Under the strings of sparkling white lights, with another bouquet of flowers and a thick picnic blanket spread across the deck, the boat looked less like a dive launch and more suited to romance. He had a bottle of wine, a small feast ready to go and a bundle of nerves in his gut. When had this become so much more than a thoughtful gesture?

He liked her. She liked him. They were friends. If he had any decent sense of timing, that would be enough. Yet the more time he spent with her, the more he wanted.

She gave his hand a squeeze and carefully stepped forward, admiring all the details. "David, this is fabulous. I don't… No one's ever…" She fanned her face with her hands. "Don't mind me. It's fabulous," she said again. "You packed a picnic?"

He nodded. "We can eat here or…" His voice trailed off, his words forgotten as the lights danced in her hair and set her skin glowing. He lost his train of thought, mesmerized by her.

"Or…" she prompted, watching him curiously.

He cleared his throat. "I had a different spot in mind," he said, thinking of the inlets behind the nearby plantations that had been turned into tourist attractions. "If you're willing to picnic on the water."

Her eager smile gave him her answer before the words left her mouth. "Yes. Let's go!"

"Have a seat, then. Do you want a glass of wine before we go?"

"No, thanks. I'm too excited. Can I help?"

He gave her heels a dubious look, but they were so sexy he was reluctant to ask her to take them off. "Sure. Can you get the bowline?"

He stifled the groan as she moved forward, the soft fabric of her dress clinging to her backside as she bent low to cast off.

With the picnic basket and cushions secured, he cast off the stern line and eased away from the dock. She surprised him, choosing to sit beside him in the wheelhouse rather than relax in the space he'd created for her.

He saw her shiver as the first chilly breeze came over the bow. "Cold?"

"Only a bit."

"There's a blanket behind your seat."

She twisted around, found it and wrapped it over her shoulders. "You thought of everything."

He laughed. "I tried." As they cleared the no-wake zone, he pushed the throttle just enough for a smooth ride across the water. He didn't want her to feel battered by the evening; he wanted her to enjoy herself. He wanted her to enjoy being with him.

He shook off the errant thought. Whatever happened in the days to come, tonight was about showing her she had significant value beyond her career and thankless job as a compassionate sister.

The first evening stars were dotting the sky as he motored up the Ashley River to a secluded spot with a superb view of Charleston. He cut the motor and dropped the anchor, leaving the lights on for safety. And mood, he thought, gazing at her lovely face.

"Ready for dinner?" he asked, helping her to her feet.

She nodded, following him without saying a word.

They settled on the cushions, the soft scent of lilies and roses mingling with the rich aroma of the wine when he poured for both of them. He unpacked the picnic, relishing her enthusiasm for the Brie and crackers, and the fruit and pasta salad. Her laughter bubbled over when she saw the box of barbecue sliders.

"This is absolutely wonderful," she said, her legs stretched out and her full plate balanced on her lap. "I can't remember a better evening."

Neither could he.

"How'd you find this place?" she asked, popping a bite of pasta salad into her mouth.

"I've been exploring ever since I moved here." He pointed to the bend in the river. "Magnolia Gardens is just up that way."

She turned to look, the loose waves of her hair sliding over her shoulder. "Impressive. I had this image of you scuba diving in every spare minute."

How had she learned to read him so well? "There's plenty to discover above the waterline." Like this woman working her way deeper into every part of him with each passing moment.

They ate in a companionable silence for several more minutes.

"Tell me a secret about you," he said, his gaze on the sky. It was too early to see any familiar constellations.

She gave a nervous laugh. "I don't have any."

"We all do," he countered, undeterred.

"Then you go first."

He shook his head. "I asked first. Come on," he urged, scooting close and putting his arm around her shoulders. "What happens on the boat stays on the boat."

Her laughter drifted up into the night sky. "I don't know about that. I want to tell everyone about this amazing date."

"Can I talk you out of that?" he asked. "I don't know if my rep can take that kind of abuse."

"Oh, please. Your rep is safe with me." She snuggled closer to him, but her voice was somber. She sipped her wine. "A secret, huh?"

He nodded, brushing his cheek across her hair as he did so.

"Being with you makes me happy."

"That's a secret?"

She looked up at him, her eyes full of emotions he couldn't label. "People think I'm happy, that I found a way to move on, but it was mostly an act."

"Really?" He knew she missed her parents,

had a tough road with Trey, but even he'd thought she was a generally happy person.

She brushed her fingertips along his chin. "Really. Life was okay, I was figuring out how to be content on my own. And then you became my friend. Spending time with you has reminded me what real happiness feels like."

He didn't know what to say. He wasn't sure he knew what to do. Something broke loose in his chest. "Terri—"

"And there I go, spoiling the mood." She started to shift away. "I swear I'm not trying to pressure you."

"*Pressure* isn't the right word," he said, holding her close. He felt weightless. "And I owe you a secret."

A shy smile curved her lips. "Do tell."

The words got caught somewhere between his brain and his mouth. There were so many things he could say, and all of them would scare her away. He took her hand and placed it over his heart. "When you smile, my heart races."

Her lips parted on a gasp and he kissed her, his tongue stroking hers. She tasted of wine and sweet berries and the night air surrounding them. He lost his breath, his pulse pounding as she kissed him back. The boat swayed gently beneath them as he pulled her across his outstretched legs, her skirt riding high on her thighs.

She broke away, her fingers gripping his shoulders as he smoothed his hands along her bared legs, higher over the curve of her hips. He'd never forget this moment, never forget how stunning she was under the canopy of soft white light and distant stars. "God, you're amazing."

He didn't care that it wasn't supposed to happen this way. He was done fighting the waves of attraction and need whenever he looked at her.

"You, too," she whispered, her lips tender and warm on his.

She made him weak, a strange sensation when he thought he could conquer anything that tried to hurt her. He surged up, wrapping her tight in his arms and easing her down to the blanket.

She gasped, her legs tangling with his as she worked open the buttons of his shirt. He pushed her hair back, nuzzling her neck and running kisses along the gentle slope of her shoulder. *More.* It was his only thought, as he found the pulse point at the hollow of her throat.

More. He tugged aside the fabric of her dress, seeking better access to her luscious body. The lace of her bra lit a fire in his veins, and he followed the gentle scallops with his tongue. He teased the hard peak of her nipple through the fabric. She arched up, a little moan of pleasure ending on his name.

He wanted all of her right now, right here.

The boat swayed, reminding him where they were and why. He leaned back, pulling her dress back into place. Better to wait, though it might kill him. "Terri, wait." David struggled for control, for rational thought as need and longing pounded through his blood. Her body, warm and pliant under his hands, was too inviting, too much temptation for any sane man. "We—we shouldn't do this here."

"We should do it somewhere," she said on a heavy sigh.

The boat rocked a little as she sat up and pushed at her hair. He laughed, surprised he could under the circumstances. "I agree."

"Then why stop?"

He closed his eyes, leaning into the caress as she stroked her fingers through his hair, careful to avoid his stitches. He couldn't remember the appeal of a military cut anymore.

"This isn't the right place." And she'd hate him if she ever learned why he'd befriended her.

She looked at him, her bewildered expression making him ache. He couldn't resist, pausing to kiss her again. "Our first time shouldn't be impulsive." He found the blanket and pulled it around her shoulders. Hiding her would never be enough distraction, not after he'd tasted her sweet skin. "Or outside in December. It should be special."

"David." She waved a hand to encompass the picnic. "This is special. No one's ever done anything like this for me."

"It's a dive boat, Terri."

"And?"

And it was damn hard to think of the right excuses and explanations when his body sided with her. "Someone could interrupt us any minute."

She glanced around. "I suppose."

"Not to mention we have to work tomorrow."

"Sure."

"Hey," he said, and tilted her face toward his. "I want you." Too much. "I don't want you ending up with regrets or second thoughts."

"I was enjoying not having any thoughts beyond you," she admitted.

"Me, too." He pushed her hair behind her ears. "You can help me drive us back."

She agreed with a tight nod. When he had things secured, he turned off the white lights and brought her body between his and the wheel at the console. It was the best sort of torture as he wrapped his arms around her, his hands guiding hers on the controls as they returned to the marina.

TERRI ENJOYED THE driving lesson surrounded by the warmth of David's tough body. If this was as close as she could get to him she'd take it. For now.

She wanted more, was sure he did, too. She was less confident about how hard she could push him. He had a valid point. Their first time should be special. Obviously, her brain was still a little scrambled after those mind-blowing kisses and the feel of his hot, powerful hands. Was she deluding herself? Was she infusing their brief friendship with more emotion than really existed?

She didn't think so. Not from her side anyway. In recent years she'd had plenty of time and counseling to accurately evaluate her feelings. It wasn't just physical desire. Yes, she had needs she'd ignored. This was more. She wanted *David* because they could laugh and talk and relax together. She trusted him.

When they reached her house and Trey's motorcycle was conspicuously absent, Terri nearly let out a grateful cheer. She shouldn't be that relieved, but she wasn't up for another confrontation. He'd told her he was staying with Cade tonight, but she'd expected him to change his mind.

She stared at the front window, at the sparkling Christmas tree. She thought of the mistletoe tied per Barnhart tradition to the light fixture in the foyer. "Will you come in?" She couldn't imagine why she felt so shy, considering what they'd been doing on his boat less than an hour ago.

"Terri—"

"Trey won't be home tonight." She felt David tense up at the mention of her brother. "He and I agreed he'd be happier at his friend Cade's place."

"Problems?"

She shrugged. Talking about Trey would kill her mood, and she wasn't ready to let go of the warm, sensual energy lingering between them. "Trey and I will figure it out at some point. Right now I'm not ready to say good-night." No, she was eager to pick up where they'd left off. He hadn't wanted to do anything impulsive, which was more than she could say for most guys. If she hadn't spent the past half hour in the car, a little tipsy from the wine and breathing in his masculine scent, she might appreciate his thoughtful restraint.

She wouldn't label what she felt now as impulsive. No, this was an intense longing only David could satisfy. The attraction couldn't be one-sided, she couldn't be that dense and he couldn't be that good at acting. Their friendship had simply shifted to something…more.

He opened his car door and came around to open hers. She felt his eyes on her legs as she swiveled around and stepped out, her body a whisper away from his. Could he hear her heart pounding? Could he feel her pulse racing as he held her hand on the short walk to her front door?

She unlocked the door and pushed it open. The glow of the Christmas tree in the family room cast a soft light into the hallway. Giving his hand an encouraging squeeze, she backed through the open doorway.

He held firm on the other side of the threshold until their arms were extended between them. "I should go."

She studied his face, so serious now. What had happened to the lighthearted man who'd planned this perfect night? "Come inside," she whispered. "Please?" She drew him closer until their linked hands were behind her back and he was standing in the foyer. She looked up, chuckling when he groaned.

"Mistletoe?" He reached back and closed the door.

"It's a lasting tradition for a reason," she whispered against his lips, hoping he'd stay.

He kissed her, the moment stretching out until her head was spinning. "I'll still respect you in the morning," she promised, breathless.

His deep laughter transformed his face as the tension lifted. "I don't want to lose your friendship."

"Me, either," she admitted. She steeled herself

for the rejection, but she wasn't backing down. "On the boat," she sucked in a breath, "it felt like you wanted me."

"I do." His hands roamed from her waist to her hips and back up again.

"Then stay. I don't want to waste any more time wondering."

"About me?"

Her heart took flight as he pulled her toward him. "About anything." She combed his hair back from his face and pressed her lips to his. The wild scents of the river and harbor clung to his clothing, washing over her as she breathed him in.

Suddenly, he broke away from her. "You're sure?"

She nodded, licking her lips and savoring the dark taste of him.

He locked the door and then scooped her into his arms. She laughed as he carried her straight through the house and up the stairs. She wasn't about to argue, though she'd had a nice little fantasy going of making love under the Christmas tree.

"Which room?" he asked.

"Second door on the right," she replied, her pulse dancing in her veins. This was happening. Light-headed, she giggled when he set her gently on her feet at the edge of her bed.

But he didn't kiss her, his breath the only movement as he seemed frozen in place. "David?" She couldn't make out his expression at all in the nearly dark room. She reached for the lamp on the nightstand.

"Don't," he said.

"Okay." She had no idea what was wrong or how to fix it.

His fingers trailed over her shoulder, down her arm. He turned her palm up and lifted her hand to his lips, kissing the pad on each of her fingers. It was outrageously arousing and she trembled with anticipation.

"Cold?"

"You know I'm not," she replied, reaching for the knot of his tie.

"Good." He caught her hand, trapped it against his chest. He kissed her, his hand working the zipper at her back as his mouth ravished hers.

If things had been hot on the boat, she was burning for him now. She put her hands under his jacket, pushed it off his broad shoulders. "I want to feel you," she murmured into the dark.

His laughter, rippling across her skin, was sinful. "Me first," he said, tugging her dress down and away. His hands caressed her body, shaped her, drawing her close enough that his erection pressed against her hip.

She worked his tie loose, then the buttons of

his shirt, desperate need spurring her on until she felt those warm, sculpted muscles under her hands.

He eased her to the bed and removed her shoes, then stripped away the rest of his clothes before he stretched out over her. For a moment, he hesitated again and she thought he'd changed his mind. He whispered her name; then his mouth found hers, and she knew there'd be no more thinking.

Her hands roamed over him, seeking and learning every angle of his chiseled body. Breathless, she arched into him as he slid her bra aside. With fingers, tongue and teeth, he teased her aching breasts. She clutched his shoulders as one sensation after another set her body sizzling from head to toe.

He kissed his way down her belly, slowly removing her lacy panties, the last barrier between them. In the dark, he moved over her once more, her sexiest fantasies come to life as he placed soft kisses to her knee and then higher, until his mouth met her core.

She cried out as his tongue, hot and urgent, pushed her to a fast, hard climax. She reached that peak, calling his name. He answered her with more of those tender, drugging kisses, his hands soothing her quivering body.

With an unexpected intensity, she wanted him

inside her. She sat up, needing to touch him, to share this pleasure surging through her. He let her take over, understanding her desire without saying a word. She thought his masculine scent alone might carry her to another orgasm as she explored his body in the dark.

He groaned as she wrapped her hand around his erection, her lips following the ripple of his abs. Suddenly she was on her back, laughing, and David was looming over her. "Maybe next time," he rasped, settling between her thighs and entering her in one smooth, satisfying thrust.

For a prolonged moment neither of them moved. Full of him, she'd never felt so much indescribable joy. She'd had sex. *This* was different. This was a thousand times better. When he started moving inside her, slowly at first, she caught his rhythm. She clutched the bunched muscles in his arms, then smoothed her hands over his back and wrapped her legs snug around his lean hips.

She didn't want it to end. Ever.

Each breath, each touch, revealed another sensual discovery, yet she felt as if she'd known this, known him, all her life.

Their pace increased, their mingled breath grew ragged, and she pressed hot kisses to the strong column of his throat. The climax shuddered from his body through hers. *Perfect* was too tame a word. *Beautiful* too extravagant. Their lovemaking had simply been…right. Long moments later, on a soft sigh, he eased his body to the side, tucking her close.

He kissed her hair as she curled into him. Her leg over his, her hand at his waist, she'd never felt so cherished.

6:15 a.m.

TERRI WOKE WITH her familiar alarm and the unfamiliar sensation of David's arm draped across her waist. As the night came back to her, she smiled. She felt absolutely blissful. Carefully, she slipped out of bed to grab a shower. If she lingered, if she paused to steal one kiss, she knew she'd be late for her shift in Franklin's ward.

As it was, David was awake and half-dressed and more tempting than ever when she returned from the shower. "Good morning," he said, his voice rough from sleep.

"Hi," she managed, mesmerized by the beard shading his jaw and his ripped torso. She caught a discoloration on his side. "What's this?"

"More evidence I can't manage in the dark."

She caught her lip between her teeth. "You did all right last night," she said, though she knew he was referring to the blackout.

He smiled. "I had better terrain to cover last night." He buttoned his shirt and looped his tie around his neck as he crossed the room for a quick embrace.

"Breakfast?" she offered, tugging on the ends of his tie.

"If you've got time."

For him, she'd make the time.

Downstairs in the kitchen he kissed her, distracted her from breakfast prep. It felt so easy, as if they did this every morning while the coffee brewed. She heard the front door open, and David's body tensed under her hands. "It's just Trey," she said, wishing she could laugh it off. "Relax," she teased. "I'm the big sister. That gives me an edge."

"Not from a brother's perspective," he replied, but he kept his arm around her waist as Trey walked into the kitchen.

"Good morning, Trey." She was determined to keep this civil.

"Looks like it might be for you." He glared at David and shook his head at Terri. "Didn't know you still had sleepovers," he said, opening the refrigerator.

She was not going to do this now and not in front of David.

"Speak to her with respect," David said.

Trey closed the refrigerator and glared at him.

"Or what? You'll make me?" He sneered. "That won't end well for you." He looked to Terri. "I can't believe you're into this guy."

"That's enough. Both of you," she warned, stepping between them. She smacked Trey on the arm with her free hand as she turned David toward the front door.

"You deserve better from him," David said. "I'll wait and drive you in."

"No, thanks." She searched for patience— with both of them. "I can handle this." She was used to Trey's surly attitude, though it was high time he found another coping mechanism. "And I have my car, remember?"

"If you're sure." He paused in the open door-way, his expression so intense her body responded, firing up all over again. "Be careful," he said, his lips soft at her ear. "You don't really know your brother anymore."

The comment doused her persistent romantic ideas and she followed him out onto the porch. "What are you basing that on?" she demanded.

"You."

His response was so unexpected she felt confused. "I'm not following."

"You've told me how things were growing up here," David continued, waving a hand toward the house. "He doesn't act at all like the brother you described."

"I—" She didn't know what to say to that.

"If you need something, anything, I'm here. Friends or lovers, that won't change. Remember that."

He turned on his heel and walked away before she found her voice.

Chapter Eleven

Friday, December 13, 7:00 a.m.

David drove back to his place, eager to spend the day staking out Terri's house and tailing Trey as needed. With her protected by the team at the hospital, he felt it was the best use of his time.

He needed to do something to keep himself from dwelling on the previous evening. Being with Terri had been damn close to perfect—before her brother had shown up snarling. No, that hadn't changed his feelings at all. It only made him more determined to protect her. Whichever way he turned it around, he couldn't imagine making a scene like that with his sisters. Teasing was one thing, but what Trey had implied? That was unforgivable.

David left his car in the driveway, just to make life easy on Trey if the jerk decided to try something stupid. Walking through the front door, he hesitated, catching a whiff of fresh-brewed coffee. Slowly, he eased open the drawer of the entry table where he stowed a pistol.

"You won't need that," a familiar voice called from the direction of the kitchen.

David kept the pistol anyway, striding through the house to find Director Casey waiting for him at his kitchen table with a full cup of coffee.

"Sir?"

"Late-night stakeout?" Casey asked.

"Not exactly," David replied, sure the director knew where he'd been. Probably what he was doing, as well, but David wouldn't tarnish Terri's reputation by elaborating on those details.

"Have a seat and relax, David. I've been in the field and I know there are challenges and consequences. I'm not judging your methods as long as the mission is foremost in your mind."

"Yes, sir." David suspected they both knew the mission hadn't been on his mind at all for several hours overnight. He was grateful he'd managed to get Terri upstairs and away from the bugs he'd planted at her house. When all hell broke loose—and his gut instinct told him that was coming—he didn't want her embarrassed, too. "You did place me here on a lifetime op."

"I did." Casey smoothed a hand down his silk tie.

David became acutely aware of his own disheveled appearance. His tie was loose around his neck, his shirt buttoned but untucked, and his slacks were creased in all the wrong places.

"Being in a permanent situation," Casey said, "you have to make different choices than you might on a temporary operation."

David nodded his agreement. He didn't have anything else to add to that assessment.

"As of last night, we've been forced to upgrade the threat level here. There's lots of chatter, but nothing definitive. The team is on the ground, watching potential sites and waiting for guidance."

David set the gun on the counter and poured himself a cup of coffee. He leaned back against the countertop and waited for the other shoe to drop. "Am I off the case?"

"No. Just the opposite, in fact. You'll take the lead when Keller strikes."

David tried to hide his relief, but he was sure Casey noticed anyway.

The director shifted in his chair. "Last night a fire department was robbed while they were out on call," he began. "Turnout gear for three firefighters is missing, along with a hazmat suit."

"From a Charleston fire department house?"

Casey shook his head. "From a neighborhood department about twenty miles away."

"What about the call they answered?"

"They were responding to a car fire at the home of one of the nurses injured earlier."

"You suspect Barnhart is behind it?"

"We have a report of a motorcycle in the area, but we don't have a solid ID at this time. What we do have is another destroyed vehicle that previously had access to the MUSC parking garage, along with plenty of chatter about targets around Charleston."

David knew Casey wouldn't be here personally if there wasn't something bigger going on. "The hospital is on the list. Dr. Palmer's project?"

"Not by name, but yes," Casey said. "Dr. Palmer and the patient have agreed to take the next step earlier than anticipated. The best-case scenario is that Keller is coming after the new biotechnology and making sure his team can get in and out swiftly."

"Redundancies and disguises," David said. "And the worst case?" he asked, afraid he knew the answer.

"Assassination of Dr. Palmer."

"Bold." It wasn't what Keller was known for, but that didn't mean he wouldn't take on a lucrative job. "Does he have some way to use the technology Dr. Palmer's developing?"

"I'm sure he thinks so. Or he has a buyer who believes they can reverse engineer it."

"But it's *in* the patient, right?"

"So I've been told." Casey's nod was somber. "Earlier devices were external or resembled a contact lens." He sipped his coffee. "I'd like to review the other potential targets. It's possible attacking the hospital is secondary to a bigger strike. Keller likes to make a statement."

"Typically hit men don't run in packs of five," David said.

"That, too."

"Hang on." David went to the small coat closet and popped out a panel hidden by the doorjamb. He retrieved a long tube of maps he'd marked up and assembled during the early weeks of his assignment to Charleston.

"I knew I put the right man on this job," Casey said, helping him unroll the maps. They pinned the corners with their coffee cups and handguns.

David started outlining the risk and reward for strikes at various locations around town, starting with areas close to the hospital. As he'd told Terri last night, he'd set out to learn more than the job and immediate community. He'd been digging into Charleston's past and present, learning all he could so he'd be prepared for any scenario.

For several minutes they discussed how and where Keller could attack with three fake fire-fighters. A team that small could infiltrate just about any fire scene.

"A fire won't get out of hand easily," David said. "The historical landmarks are well protected." He thought of the test-run attack on Dr. Palmer's ward and tried to envision a scene involving firemen. "The blackout didn't result in an evacuation, but a fire—a real one—would."

"That's my first concern. It would force Dr. Palmer and the patient out of the building."

"Setting a fire in that ward is almost impossible."

"Almost?"

"Few things are impossible." David shifted the maps, revealing the blueprints for the hospital. "After the blackout, security is tighter than ever. Keller would have to hit a floor above or below. Even dressed as firefighters, the men would need ironclad identification to get close enough to cause problems," David said.

Casey agreed. "We'll keep monitoring. I believe Keller will strike soon. I've put the Weapons Station and other possible targets on alert."

David rolled up the blueprints and maps, tapping them back into the tube and hiding them again. "I'll stick close to the Barnharts."

Casey stood and moved toward the door. "Keller might very well plan to use one to leverage the other. Keep your phone on."

"Always, sir," David replied as Casey walked out.

He scrubbed his hand through his hair, swearing when he bumped his stitches. It was an uncomfortable reminder that he'd been bested by Keller's team once already. "Fool me once," he muttered, heading upstairs to shower and change clothes for work.

There was a way to anticipate and intercept Keller. There had to be. Terri as the target felt much different than Terri as someone in the wrong place at the wrong time. It might be casual Friday, but there was nothing casual about David's urgent need to see that she was safe.

An hour later, David walked up to the security guard stationed outside Franklin's ward and handed over his hospital ID. "I'd like to see Terri Barnhart."

"I'll check on that." The security guard gave him a hard look as he radioed the request to the nurses station inside. David knew he was being watched through the closed-circuit camera in the corner. "She'll be right out," the guard said after a moment.

David waited, hiding his impatience. His eyes drifted over the fresh paint and glossy floors in front of the nurses station that had been attacked. His stomach pitched. Terri could very well find herself in the middle of Keller's next attempt to seize Dr. Palmer's new device.

When the doors parted, David grinned, despite the little pucker of a frown between her eyebrows. "Hey," he said.

"Hey yourself," she replied, walking farther from the guard station. "What brings you by?"

He shrugged. "Just checking in." He could see her trying to suppress a smile and he hoped that was a good sign. "We didn't exactly part on the best of terms this morning. I wanted to apologize."

"It's okay. I know your heart's in the right place."

Maybe he should've given her a stronger warning. Better yet, maybe he should just come clean. "Did your brother give you hell?"

"He tried," she said. "You might've noticed I'm an adult."

"I've noticed more than that."

"Hush." A blush colored her cheeks. "I'm fine."

"I noticed that, too," he said, putting himself between her and the guard. "Are we okay?"

She nodded.

"Good. Come by my place tonight. I'll cook."

"You did all that for me last night," she said with a siren's smile. "It's my turn to cook, but I can't tonight." Her gaze slid away from his.

"You need to be with your brother." He filled in the words she seemed reluctant to say. He rubbed her shoulders when she tensed up. "I get it. What kind of jerk would I be if I made you choose?"

"Thanks for understanding. I know you don't have any reason to believe me, but Trey wasn't always such an idiot."

He chuckled, running his hands up and down her arms. "He cares about you." David hoped it was true. He wanted to warn her about the threats to the hospital, about her brother's likely actions last night, but that had backfired every time. The best he could do was make sure she had no reason to be irritated or concerned about his involvement with her.

"What time are you off?"

"We could run late up here today," she said.

Her evasion was so obvious. Even if Casey hadn't mentioned Dr. Palmer's plans, David would've known that was the answer Security had told her to give.

"Come over."

Her eyes were warm as she gazed up at him.

"You drive right by my place on your way home," he cajoled. If she didn't agree soon, he might resort to begging. "Just for a few minutes. So I can hold you without anyone glaring at me." He raised his chin in the direction of the guard.

"I'm not sure a few minutes will be enough."

"Talk like that will plague me all day," he confessed.

"At least I won't suffer alone."

"I don't want you to suffer at all," he replied with absolute sincerity. "If there's anything you need, call me."

"You keep saying that."

"Because it's true." The desire shining in her eyes drew him in, and it was all he could do to keep his lips from hers. Only the knowledge of everyone watching this drama play out kept him in line. He didn't ever want to be a source of embarrassment for her. He hoped she'd remember these moments, remember his sincerity, if he ever had to tell her his real purpose here.

"I, uh, have to get back to work," she stammered. She didn't move.

"Right." He smiled at her, smoothing a wayward wisp of her hair back behind her ear. "Have a good day."

AFTER DAVID'S VISIT, Terri's day perked up. She'd been concerned David would agree with Trey's obnoxious conclusion that she didn't have room for both men in her life. Change—good or bad— had always been challenging for her brother. At some point he had to grow up and deal with it. Seeing her as a woman couldn't be easy, but it was a fact of life. Her life.

She should've asked for Trey's key after he implied her judgment was impaired by David's body. When she got home, they would hash this out once and for all. Childhood home or not, if he couldn't show respect, he couldn't stay at the house. She could almost hear her mother's voice encouraging patience, reminding her they were family despite disagreements.

Terri kept one eye on the clock, the other on the chart as she waited for Franklin to emerge from the operating suite. Doctor and patient had been prepped and excited as they moved decisively toward the final step in the project.

She thought of Matt and Franklin, knowing how desperately each man wanted this device to succeed. She admired them for funneling their grief into something functional and positive. She'd thought she'd done that, redirecting her grief into stabilizing Trey, helping him move forward with new goals, but now she wasn't sure.

What had been a bad mood last night before her date had been downright nasty this morning. She didn't want David to be right, didn't want to believe that something she couldn't understand had changed Trey when he'd disappeared.

Was she simply mirroring Trey's resistance to change? The thought startled her.

"Miss Barnhart?"

She glanced up when the security guard called her name over the intercom. "Yes?"

"You have another visitor. Says he's your brother."

Her light mood was eclipsed by a looming thundercloud. "Good grief," she muttered. She wanted to ignore the summons, but that wouldn't solve anything. Look at how they'd been trying to ignore their common grief. "Call me the minute they're out of the OR," she said to Regina as she headed for the door.

Trey stood at the far end of the hallway, near the windows that looked out over an inner courtyard. Right now the garden was dormant, in various shades of faded green and dull brown branches. Stark, but she still found it lovely. In the spring, the grass would be lush and thick and the crepe myrtle trees would bloom in bright spikes of white and purple flowers.

"What do you want?" She stopped a few paces from the secure door. She'd keep an open mind, but she wanted an apology for his rude behavior this morning.

"I need a minute," Trey said.

She rolled her hand, urging him to get on with it. "A minute is about all I have."

"Did something happen?" he asked, looking past her to the locked doors.

She narrowed her gaze. "It's work." She shot her hands wide. "I am at *work*. What couldn't wait until I'm off shift?"

"I wanted to talk with you privately." He took a step closer, pausing when she glared at him. "Come on. I'm your brother."

"Uh-huh."

"You took time to chat with your new boyfriend."

Terri's jaw dropped. "You've been watching me?"

A tense muscle in Trey's jaw jumped. "I've been watching *over* you."

Lord, save her. "In case you haven't noticed, I'm in the most secure part of the building. Go away. They shouldn't have let you up here."

"You should listen to me."

She wished he'd listen to her. "Say something worth hearing."

Trey rushed forward and caught her by the arm. "Let go of me," she said.

"I am trying to be discreet," Trey muttered. "Your new boyfriend is not an HR lackey."

"I know." She wrenched her elbow free of his grip, catching herself before she plowed that elbow into his ribs. "We'll talk about it at home."

Trey looked shocked. "He told you?"

"Contrary to popular belief, I don't report to you. I'm a big girl and while your concern is appreciated, it's not necessary. David is good to me. He's good *for* me."

"So he didn't tell you," Trey said with a sneer. "Your Mr. Good Guy is a spy. He's playing you."

"Trey, I swear—"

"He's using you and you're letting him."

Trey's words landed like a sledgehammer and, though she tried, she couldn't defend herself. "Of all the childish displays." She swallowed back the surge of tears as anger and insecurity went to war inside her. She would not dismiss the best thing in her life because her brother was being an ass. "You don't get to talk to me that way. Especially not at work. Go home. No. Go to Cade's—"

"Martin is a spy. I have evidence."

"Of what?" She pressed her hands to her eyes. David a spy. It was absurd. "He's new in town, Trey. That's all."

"Where was he during the blackout?"

"In the dark with the rest of us." She rolled her eyes and turned on her heel. "I'm going back to work."

But Trey caught her again and put his face close to hers. "He *caused* the blackout."

The security guard watched them, his stony face impassive. "Are you okay, Miss Barnhart?"

"Yes, thank you." She could handle her

brother. "Trey," she said, keeping her voice low as warning. "You need to leave."

He jerked back as though she'd slapped him. Obviously they both knew she wanted to. "You need to believe me. He's dangerous."

This time she caught his arm, forcing him away from the entrance doors. They already thought he was a security risk, and this wasn't helping her stay on the job. A job she wanted to finish now that she was involved. "We'll talk about it later. You're embarrassing me."

"Better that than to hear you're a casualty. Come home with me, Terri."

"I can't walk out on a shift," she replied, shocked that he would suggest such a thing.

"You're playing with fire," Trey said. "Think about it. How did your boyfriend get that cut on his head?"

She refused to play along with his bizarre theory. "I can't believe you'd do this." She drilled a finger into his chest and drove him back until the wall prevented his escape. "I'm happy for the first time since, since..." She forced herself to say it. "Since our parents died." There. The world didn't end. "I'm feeling normal, having a normal life again, and you just can't stand it, can you?"

"That's not it, I swear. Of course I want you happy."

"That's why you disappeared without as

much as a text message? You were thinking of *me* when you dropped out, tossing away the opportunity you worked so hard for?"

"*You* worked for that. You wanted me to go to college."

"Don't even try that. No one forced you out. You found the programs. You filled out the applications. You were excited on move-in day."

"I'm back now and I want what's best for you."

"Oh, please. What's best for me is letting me do my job."

"It will always come first, won't it?"

"I didn't make the world, Trey, I just live in it. By the rules," she added with another poke to his chest. "I'm not going to lose my job because you're going through—" she flicked her hands at him "—whatever this is."

"It's too much to take time off to be with me, but that guy snaps his fingers and you're dressed to kill?"

She gasped and a chill skated over her skin. She hadn't dressed until after Trey left last night. Why was he watching her like some kind of stalker? "I'm happy to arrange for time off to be with you. I just have to give a little notice."

"Right." Trey folded his arms across his chest. "You had a day off and came rushing back here."

"Franklin needed me," she said defensively. "You told me you had work to do anyway."

"That's different."

Exasperated, she glanced at the security guard and for a moment imagined having him escort her brother off the property. It might be the only way to get through a shift in peace. "I really need to get back to work."

"Come downstairs with me and ask Mr. Perfect yourself."

"Enough, Trey. Just drop it. David's a normal guy and I like him. I won't let you come between us."

Trey laughed, the sound humorless. "You're blind." He reached into his pocket. "And stubborn. You're not always right."

She bit back the sharp retort. She was certainly feeling wrong about her brother.

"He's a spy," Trey continued. "I'm not sure who he works with, but he's targeted you."

Wishing she could curl up and cover her ears, she tucked her hands into her pockets, hiding her clenched fists. "Get it out. Just say what's on your mind so I can get back to work. You may not care, but I love my job."

"Terri, you're going to get hurt if you don't come with me right now. Why can't you give me the benefit of the doubt?"

Because I've given you too much already. Years of love, support and energy. Endless encouragement. Boundless hope. In return, he'd given her worry and stress. She kept all that bottled up tight inside. This wasn't the time or place to spew her frustration. "He makes me happy, Trey. It's going to take more than these wild claims to change my mind."

David had never been anything but a good friend. Supportive, kind, fun. Romantic when things took that turn. Based on last night, they were more than compatible on every possible level. She wouldn't let her brother ruin it.

"I didn't want to do this," Trey declared. He handed her a small plastic bag with three tiny objects inside.

"What's this?"

"Bugs. Covert listening devices," he added. "I broke them."

He couldn't mean… She looked up into her brother's hooded gaze. "Why are you carrying these around?"

"Because I didn't want them in *our* house anymore. That's the second set I found since I got back."

"My house," she mumbled. It wasn't a correction as much as an expression of confusion. Someone had been inside her house? Someone had been listening to her daily routine? "That's not possible."

"It is. Ask your boyfriend about them."

"David didn't have anything to do with this."

"Someone did."

She stared at the devices, confused and concerned that her brother would resort to such drastic measures to get between her and David.

"Dr. Palmer is asking for you," the security guard said, cutting through her haze.

"Thank you," Terri replied. "I'll be right there." To Trey, she said, "We'll talk when I get home."

"Come with me now or I won't be there." He shoved a hand into his pocket. "If you won't trust me, it's not home for me anymore."

"Your choice." The words, the only possible response, took their toll. "I can't walk out on this shift."

Trey swore. "I'd get more of your attention if I was a patient."

She watched him stalk away, heard his feet pounding on the treads before the stairwell door closed behind him. Would the emotional blackmail ever stop with him?

Tucking the plastic bag deep into her pocket, she promised herself she'd research the devices after her shift and try to figure out what in the world her brother was up to.

Bugging the house made no sense. She was a nurse, with few connections and limited access to anything important. Until Franklin had asked her to fill in, she'd had no idea anything with a military application was being studied here.

If Trey had pulled these from her house, whoever was listening must be vastly disappointed. Living alone, she didn't have anyone to discuss work with. She didn't even have a pet right now, though she'd been considering adopting a cat as a Christmas present for herself.

The security guard stopped her at the door as he swiped her ID badge through the reader. "You okay?"

She nodded. "My brother is struggling. It's seasonal," she fibbed. "If he comes back, send him away." Franklin was counting on her to do her job without distractions. "Barring famine or flood, I'll see him at home tonight."

"Yes, ma'am."

Terri walked in and saw Franklin in the kitchenette, beaming as he waited for a cup of coffee to brew. "Everything went well?" she asked.

"Flawlessly," Franklin said. "Matt will be out of recovery within the hour and we can start testing."

"Wonderful."

He added a spoonful of sugar to his mug and stirred it. "Can I have a word?" he asked as they left the kitchen.

She followed him into the office and closed

the door at his request. "I don't want anyone else to hear this," he explained.

She waited, her fingertips fiddling with the plastic bag in her pocket. Hopefully, Trey hadn't lied about breaking the devices.

"One of the nurses on the team was attacked last night."

"Again?" Terri sat down hard in the nearest chair. "Is she okay? What happened?"

"Her car was set on fire in her driveway."

Terri shook her head. "That's terrible."

"My security staff had her under surveillance as a safety precaution. They report hearing a motorcycle in the neighborhood shortly before the attack."

"Are you suggesting Trey had something to do with it?" She wanted to be outraged by the accusation; instead, she worried Franklin was onto something.

"I'm just asking if your brother was home with you last night."

"No." She swallowed around the lump of fear in her throat. "We had an argument, and he said he'd stay over with a friend."

Franklin pushed a pad of paper across the desk. "Can you give me the friend's name and a phone number?"

"I only have his name and the address of

where he grew up," she said, writing it down quickly. "He might be out on his own now."

"Any information you have is fine," Franklin assured her. "The security team isn't taking any chances."

"That's good." She thought of the bugs in her pocket and wondered if it was protocol to eavesdrop on the people on the project. That possibility made more sense than David being a spy. Except if Trey was telling the truth, the bugs were planted before Franklin had asked her to fill in up here.

"Terri," Franklin continued with a heavy sigh. "I'm sorry."

"For what?"

"For not explaining the full extent of the risks of being on this project. I didn't expect outright attacks on the staff. After the blackout I had no choice. I needed someone I could trust implicitly. There aren't many." He stacked his hands on the desk. "Maybe I should have expected that our success would leak, that there might be serious efforts to stop my progress. Regardless, I think you should leave. For your own safety."

She thought of everything Matt and Franklin had endured. "No, thank you."

Franklin's eyes widened, his thick eyebrows reaching for his hairline. "But I—"

"Life is risk, Franklin. I'd rather stay and make a stand against the violence."

"That's very brave," he said quietly. "But I don't want to lose another daughter."

Her heart swelled with love for the man who truly had been like a second father. "I'll manage," she promised. "Together, we'll get your research safely to the next stage."

"If you're sure."

"I am."

He didn't look thrilled with her determination, but she chalked that up to fear of more loss. She knew from experience it was a result of losing loved ones early and suddenly.

He pushed back from the desk. "All right." His smile didn't quite reach his eyes. "Let's go see how our patient is doing."

She followed him out, a strange mix of curiosity and concern brewing in her belly. At least it kept her mind off the broken bugs in her pocket. It seemed she didn't know anyone as well as she thought she did. Not her brother, her friend or her new lover. It would be silly to talk to David about the bugs and yet she knew she had to. Not for Trey, but for her own peace of mind.

Chapter Twelve

At his weight bench, David adjusted the key in the stack, upping the resistance, and then he leaned back for another set of chest presses. The equipment had been a splurge, but he'd justified it. Better to have easy access at home than deal with gym hours, and training helped him think.

The new bugs in Terri's place had been disabled. For a newbie in the terrorist game, Trey was doing a decent job of thwarting law enforcement efforts. Finishing his reps, David eased the stack down and sat up, stretching his arms overhead.

Hearing the doorbell, he glanced at the clock and wiped the sweat from his face with the towel. He'd been at it for nearly an hour and wasn't any closer to feeling better about the situation. The bell rang again. "Coming!" he called out, picking up the pace.

He peered through the sidelight window and grinned at the sight of Terri on his doorstep. A tough day was looking much better. Still in her scrubs, she must've come straight from her shift. He opened the door, pleased that she'd accepted his invitation to stop by on her way home.

"Hey," he said, bending to kiss her, but she gave him her cheek instead. His instincts leaped into high gear. "What's wrong?"

"Nothing I hope." Her soft green gaze drifted over his body. "Did...did I catch you at a bad time?"

God help him, he was helpless against that curious gaze. He stepped back and motioned her in, checking the driveway and street behind her.

"We need to talk."

"Give me five minutes and I won't smell like a gym rat."

"You smell fine. I mean..." Her voice trailed off as her cheeks turned pink. "This doesn't have to take long."

"Okay. I'm all yours." He led her to the kitchen and poured them each a glass of water.

"Thanks."

"Hey." He brushed her long bangs away from her face. "Talk to me."

She closed her eyes, shaking her head before her eyes popped open once more. "I'm just going to say it and if...if I've been an idiot, well..."

An idiot? His mind raced through the possible ways she would finish that sentence. "You need something stronger than water?" He thought he might if this conversation took a wrong turn.

"No." She gulped the water, then set the glass down and met his gaze. "My brother thinks you're some kind of spy."

David hid his reaction by taking a big pull on his water, wishing it was a shot of bourbon. So what if Keller had read his background and made a few educated guesses? He'd been expecting as much. "And you think he's right because...?"

"I don't know what to think," she admitted. "Aren't you going to deny it?"

He cleared his throat. "What you believe matters more to me."

"He gave me these." She rooted through her purse and pulled out a small plastic bag, thrusting it at him.

He arched an eyebrow as he took it from her and examined the contents. It looked as though Trey had found all three of the bugs he'd planted yesterday. "Where did you get these?"

"Trey told me you planted them in my house."

David tossed the plastic bag on the countertop. "Your brother isn't my biggest fan."

"Well, no. He said you caused the blackout at the hospital."

That pissed him off. "What evidence did he use to make that case?" He ran his fingers over the knuckles he'd scraped up while fighting her brother. Terri's eyes followed the movement.

"You told me you fought a wall in the blackout," she said. "What really happened?"

He wanted to tell her that he'd followed Trey into the basement and been knocked around for daring to interfere with her brother's schemes.

"I'm the new guy in the department, right?"

She nodded.

"Every department has an emergency protocol."

"I know," she snapped.

"They put me on morgue duty," he said with a shrug. "In case of an emergency, I make sure the docs down there get out."

"Uh-huh."

She wanted to believe him; he could see it in her eyes. It was tempting to take her in his arms and distract her, but he was sweaty and as a point of pride, he wanted to win her over with logic. Even if it was logic based on untruths.

Hell, they were both lying to her. Like a little kid grasping for approval, he wanted her to believe his story over her brother's. "It wasn't a wall," he began. "I went downstairs and some guy in a dark jacket and mask attacked me. I tried to stop him, but he got away. It was too dark to make any sort of identification."

"You were in a fight?"

With her brother, but he left that out. "Barely qualifies, since I was so ineffective. Security knows about it, but I'd rather tell the wall story than admit I let the man responsible for the chaos that day get away. I'm sorry I didn't tell you sooner."

Her expression edged closer to sympathy, until her eyes landed on the bag of bugs. "And what about those?"

"I can't explain those at all." It was the truth.

"Then how did they get into my house?"

"Did you see them in your house?"

Her eyebrows drew together into a quizzical frown. "What do you mean?"

"You can pick up these things anywhere on-line or in some specialty electronic stores." He opened his arms wide, held his hands up. "I have no reason to invade your privacy with something like that." No, he just needed to invade her home to listen for news of her brother as a terrorist threat. He put a muzzle on the guilt gnawing at his conscience. "You want to know what I think?"

"Tell me."

"I think your brother's feeling possessive and out of sorts."

"You're suggesting he's making up this spy thing."

David nodded and reached for his water,

resisting the urge to cross his arms over his chest. He didn't want to show anything she could interpret as defensive body language. "I'm an HR guy," he said. "They make us take some psych classes, you know."

That got a smile out of her. "And you've analyzed my brother."

He hitched a shoulder, kept his voice light. "I'm speculating, that's all. I think he came home feeling guilty for making you worry. I think he wants things to be the way they were before your lives fell apart. He can't win back the athletic scholarships, but he can try to win over his sister."

"He never lost me," she muttered, raising her eyes to the ceiling and blinking away tears. "Why can't he understand that?"

"Boys can be dumb," he said, pleased when she agreed with a snort. "He doesn't know me and he doesn't want me around. He sees me as a threat to your relationship."

"I suppose that makes sense."

"It's a fair assessment."

"You must think I'm an idiot."

"No." Never. She was too smart for him to easily keep his secrets for much longer. "You love your brother. That's obvious. I get it."

"It sounded ridiculous, but I had to ask." She snatched the plastic bag from the countertop and walked over to throw it in the trash can. "I just... I don't know you." She blushed. "I mean, we haven't known each other long, I—" She cut herself off. "I'll just get going."

"Stay," he said, pleased when she stopped short. "I'll make dinner and we'll work on that knowing-each-other thing."

"You're too nice to me," she said. "I can't horn in on your evening."

"There's no other way I'd rather spend my evening." He realized the words, his intentions, went far beyond this conversation or even this case. He wanted to be with her for as long as she wanted him around. Which, if Rediscover used Trey as everyone expected, wouldn't be much longer. "Let me grab a shower and I'll put shark steaks on."

"You have shark steaks?"

"If you'd rather have something else or go out—"

"Shark steaks are fine." When she smiled, her eyes sparkled again.

"Great." He tugged at his damp T-shirt. "Make yourself at home." He headed for the hallway. "I'll be back in ten minutes. Unless..."

"Unless?" she echoed.

"You want to join me?"

Her eyebrows shot toward her hairline, and her lips tilted in a sexy half smile. He knew in that moment she was ready to say yes. "Next time," she managed in a husky whisper.

"Can I get that in writing in ten minutes?"

She nodded. "Sure."

David rushed through a cold shower and pulled on clean jeans and a fresh shirt. He didn't want to give her a minute longer than necessary to change her mind. It wasn't all about damage control, though his mind spun various theories about the motive behind Trey's accusations. After dinner, he would need to send an update to Casey. If Trey was pushing this hard for Terri to give him the boot, the real attack had to be coming soon.

As he walked back to the kitchen, he spotted Terri on a bar stool, flipping through one of his dive magazines. His heart banged hard against his rib cage. Who knew falling in love would feel so normal and significant all at once?

In his mind, he saw the pictures of the nurses who'd been hurt during the blackout attack. David would not let Terri become another statistic. Trey and Keller might consider him a spy, but they had no understanding of his tenacity. Not only for protecting Dr. Palmer's research, but for protecting Terri from them.

She caught him staring and turned, smiling.

"You stayed," he said. He loved her. Good

grief, he realized it was true. He loved her. It had to be too soon to tell her.

"Well, shark steak is hard to resist."

"Yeah." He walked over and leaned in close, giving her a chance to turn her cheek again.

TERRI'S PULSE SIZZLED under the tender assault of David's lips, and she gently pushed her fingers into his damp hair, holding him close. He made her feel special. Beautiful and treasured. Engulfed by his heat and strength, the brisk scent of his body wash surrounding her, she could almost forget dinner—and the rest of the world. If she could be sure it wouldn't make him run, she'd warn him that she was falling in love.

Her stomach growled, embarrassing her, and their kiss ended on a bubble of laughter. "It was a long shift," she explained. "I missed most of my lunch break."

"Can you talk about it?"

"In vague terms, I suppose. The patient is doing really well."

"That's good." He kissed her nose, then walked around her to the refrigerator.

She watched him gather ingredients and start a marinade. "What can I do to help?"

"Not a thing. Just relax."

"Hmm. Okay." It wasn't a hardship to sit and rest while he fixed dinner. Still, she felt bad for barging in, making an outrageous accusation and then letting him manage the meal. "I should go get a bottle of wine or something."

"Check the dining room. My sisters dumped a crate of housewarming supplies on me at Thanksgiving. I'm sure there's wine."

"You told me you were a beer guy." His laughter followed her into the dining room.

"The meddling matchmakers remain ever hopeful that I'll be inspired to buy a wine rack and impress the ladies."

"Ah." She didn't care for his use of the plural. After last night, in her mind and with everything in her heart, she'd moved their relationship to exclusive. That didn't mean he had to do the same, but she supposed they should talk about it. Just not now.

He hadn't been kidding about the crate. A large box made of wood slats was definitely intended as a decor piece once it was empty. It was currently stuffed with packing straw and a variety of items, including three bottles of wine. She pulled out a cabernet sauvignon and headed back to the kitchen. "How's this?"

He glanced up from chopping greens. "Whatever suits you." He winked at her. "I'm having a beer."

"I don't want to open this just for me."

"My sisters would be sad to hear that."

"But I can't drink it all with one dinner."

He walked over and leaned across the counter. "Then you'll have to come back tomorrow." He kissed one corner of her mouth. "And the day after that." He kissed the other corner. "And maybe the next night to finish it off." He met her lips once more.

"Oh." It was the best she could manage when he leaned back and looked at her that way. The passion building inside her was reflected in his gray eyes. "That's a plan."

He handed her the corkscrew and, as she opened the wine, she wished she'd stopped at the house first to change clothes. She couldn't even remember if her bra and panties matched. Probably not, since she'd dressed in a hurry in the dark, hoping to let David sleep in.

She let herself admire the view of his worn jeans hugging his backside as he turned away to finish dinner. "Is my brother a deal breaker for us?" Where had that come from? She glared at the unopened bottle of wine, unable to blame anything but her own stupidity for that question. She held up a hand when he turned to face her. "Don't answer that. It's too soon."

"Not for me," he said.

She waited, but he didn't clarify if he meant it wasn't too soon for him or if Trey wasn't a deal breaker. She didn't have the nerve to ask.

"Please give me something to do," she begged. "It will shut me up."

"Your questions don't bother me," he said, laughing. "Come over here and toss the salad."

"Thank you." Hurrying around the counter, she kept her mouth shut and her hands busy with the salad while he finished cooking the steaks.

They ate at the table, the conversation limited to minimal comments and safe topics as they devoured the food.

"That was amazing." She blotted her lips with the napkin. "Thank you so much. I'm stuffed." She started to get up, intending to take care of the dishes.

"Hang on." He caught her hand. "We haven't had dessert."

"I couldn't possibly..." Her voice trailed off when she realized he wasn't talking about food. He had that gleam in his eyes, the one she didn't want to resist. Last night in his arms, her world had spun off its axis. As much as she wanted to repeat that experience, this wasn't the right night. "David..." She cleared her throat. "I should get home. Franklin wants me in first thing tomorrow."

"Another shift?"

She nodded. "He already worked it out with my boss. After the blackout, security is tighter than ever. There are only a few of us approved by the research security team."

He stood, moving behind her. His hands were warm on her neck, and she sighed as he started massaging the tension out of her shoulders. "Just a little TLC and I'll see you home."

"I drove," she reminded him.

"Doesn't mean I can't be a gentleman."

She groaned. It made her feel even worse about telling him what her brother had said. She should've seen the jealousy behind Trey's wild claims. "I'm capable of making it home on my own."

"Of course you are," he said. "You're one of the most capable women I know. But—"

"That doesn't mean you can't be a gentleman."

"Exactly." She felt his lips replace his hands, and a delicious tremor of anticipation slid down her spine. The man could make her burn for him with the smallest attention. She really wanted to give in to that attention.

His warm breath feathered over her ear as he trailed kisses over the sensitive skin on her neck. "David."

"Right here."

She tried to get a grip on her thoughts. "I should do the dishes."

"I might let you. In a minute." His hands slid down her arms and back up again. "Come here."

A puppet would have more self-control, she thought, responding to his clever touches as he urged her up and out of the chair.

He pulled her flush against his warm, wide chest and kissed her until thoughts of brothers, dishes and deal breakers were history. She ran her hands over his shoulders, gasping as he boosted her up to sit on the countertop. He spread her knees wide and leaned in for a searing kiss.

She wrapped her legs around his hips, drawing their bodies together. Heat and desire sparked between them, around them. She'd had crazy thoughts all day long that last night had been too good—a once-in-a-lifetime thing. He was blowing holes in that theory right now.

When he cupped her breasts in his hands, she pressed into the hot touch, needing more. Tugging the hem of his shirt free from his jeans, she slid her hands up along the enticing angles and planes of his hot, firm muscles.

"Oh, David," she whispered, her head falling back as he yanked her scrub top up and away. No dessert? Who was she kidding? She was offering herself like a sundae with a cherry on top. "Do you have any whipped cream?" she heard herself ask. They were in the kitchen after all. This time she could blame the wine, though she'd only had one glass.

"I'll stock up for tomorrow," he promised, his mouth closing over her breast through the thin fabric of her camisole.

She combed her fingers through his thick, wavy hair, holding him close. She didn't know how she'd gotten so lucky to be with him, but she knew she didn't want it to end anytime soon—to hell with her brother's false worries.

She shifted, bringing his mouth back to hers. This want, this desperate need, was so new. She wanted to feel him deep inside her again when his body went tight as a bowstring. "David," she whispered against his lips, reaching for his fly. "I need—"

The shrill sound of her phone cut through the sensual fog.

"Ignore it," he suggested, laying claim to her mouth and sweeping his hot tongue across hers.

She pushed him back a fraction of an inch. Barely room to breathe. "I can't. It's the ringtone I set for the hospital."

He swore, and she agreed wholeheartedly as she fished her phone out of her purse. "Hello?"

"Terri."

Not the hospital. Her brother. What the hell? The interruption worked better than the coldest shower. "What?"

"You've got to come home." He sounded upset. "Now. I need…"

"What is it, Trey?" She was done with his theatrics. "When did you change my ringtone?"

"Now, Terri. I'm hurt. They shot me."

"Who?" Hearing the pain in his voice, she hopped off the counter. Questions could wait until she got there. "I'm on my way."

David caught her attention and rolled his eyes. She ignored him. They would work out their issues later.

"Alone, right?" Trey asked.

"Why?" Suddenly suspicious, she walked to David's front window, looking for any sign of her brother. "Is this another wild stunt?"

"No! I just don't need an audience."

"What did you do?"

"Hurry, Terri," Trey said with a grunt. "There's a lot of blood."

She ended the call and slipped her scrub top back on. "I'm sorry," she said to David. "He's hurt."

"How bad?"

"I won't know until I get there, will I? He says there's a lot of blood."

"I'll come with you."

"No." She planted her palm on his chest. "I've got this."

"Terri…"

"Capable, remember?"

"Yeah," he grumbled.

"I'll text you," she said as she raced out his front door, wondering what in the world her brother had done now.

Chapter Thirteen

Terri pulled into the driveway, urging the garage door to move faster. Trey had sounded so desperate and afraid on the phone. She tried to hold back the memories and failed. Her heart pounded and the blood rushed through her head as she remembered those first hours and days after the accident. She pushed it aside. This wasn't the time for fainting.

Trey had been fragile then. Critically injured. He was whole and healthy now. Keys in hand, she took a deep breath and forced herself to slow down as she walked into the house.

Trey might be in a strange emotional place, but he was fit and strong again. His clinginess was most likely about wanting to be the center of her world. She couldn't fault him for the expectation—she'd put her brother and his needs first from the moment they lost their parents.

"Trey?" She hooked her key ring on the rack by the door.

"Over here!" Trey's voice was tight and thready.

Terri's determination to remain calm wavered as she spotted him on the floor of the family room. She quashed the urge to assume a worst-case situation. The wound could be less serious than Trey's pained voice indicated.

The blood soaking through his shirt, smearing his hands, told a different story. "What happened?" she demanded, relying on her training as she began assessing his condition.

"They found me."

"Who did?" She helped him to his feet. "Let's get you cleaned up."

"The team," he said. "I—I went out for the mail. They were waiting. Down the block."

She grabbed a kitchen chair and settled him near the sink. "Keep talking."

"The car rolled to a stop. Between me and the house," he said. "This guy got out. Joe."

"Joe?"

"I don't know his last name. Everyone at Rediscover called him Joe."

"Hold that thought." She looked at his eyes, pleased that he appeared steady. "I'm grabbing the first-aid kit," she explained. "Don't move." She hurried away, pausing to grab her cell phone, as well as the supplies from under the sink in the powder room.

"Do I need stitches?" he asked when she returned.

"I'm about to find out," she replied. She moved his hand and snapped a quick picture of the bloodstained shirt. With scissors she cut away his sleeve, letting it drop to the floor. She wet a towel and let him wipe the blood from his hands. Soaking another towel in cool water, she started cleaning his wound. "If the bullet's inside you'll need to go to a hospital." She wasn't sure she wanted him to be seen at her hospital.

"It went straight through." Trey shifted in the chair. "I can't go to the hospital."

"Why not?"

"They have to report gunshot wounds."

True. And she'd seen her share during her shifts in the ER. "Is there some reason you don't want Joe to be found and arrested?"

"Well, yeah. If he's arrested, more people from the team will show up. They want me to go back, Terri. I can't do that."

"I thought you loved your new job and the opportunities."

"I lied," he said, his face crumpling. "I won't go back. My place is here. With you."

That sounded like an afterthought. He'd used that scared teenager voice again, but she wasn't convinced. "No one is going to make you do anything you don't want to do, least of all take you out of the state against your will. You're an adult." She wanted to ask why he'd claimed his team had been such a healing experience, only to paint them as violent now. Instead, she dealt with the immediate problem.

She examined the entry wound on the front of his arm, noting the discoloration. She wasn't a forensic expert, but it seemed Joe had shot Trey at a very close range. Gently, she prodded his arm just enough to confirm there was a clean exit wound. "You were right. Feels like the bullet went straight through."

"Good."

She didn't trust herself to agree with his opinion. Something was wrong with the angle. "Did you fight with him in the street?"

She wanted an answer that would dispel the ugly suspicions that were quickly becoming theories in her mind. It was his left arm. Trey was right-handed. The bullet, small caliber, had entered just above the midpoint of his biceps and traveled straight through. It was all a little too clean.

"He got out of the car and we argued. He pulled out a big-ass handgun and tried to grab me and shove me into the car, but I jerked away. That's when he fired."

Her heart broke, wondering if it was all lies. "You need stitches," she said, trying to sort it out.

"Go ahead," Trey said. "You can do that, right?"

"Sure, if I had a suture kit. You need a hospital."

He shook his head. "This isn't a big deal. Just wrap it up. Don't you have glue in there?"

She knocked his hand away when he started rooting through the first-aid box. "Yes, but—"

"Use that. I can't go to the hospital," he insisted.

She stood up, her gaze locked with his. "You're the victim of a crime." Even if it was likely only a weapon discharged inside city limits. "The team knows where you live. Why does it matter if you report the shooting?"

"It just does."

"You're not making any sense," she accused. He'd brought bad people right to their doorstep. Her doorstep, she amended. "I'm proud of you for escaping what is apparently a bad situation. Do the right thing and let the authorities take it from here."

"No." He grabbed her hand in a hard grip. "If I report them, it only gets worse."

She didn't want worse for either of them, but she didn't have much faith that Trey could effectively avoid armed men. Assuming they existed. In her mind, she heard the echo of David's warning. Her brother was different. Beyond the physical fitness and golden tan, he'd become a person she didn't understand. She'd seen paranoid patients, and Trey didn't quite meet that standard definition, but something was definitely off. If he'd been lying and hiding the reality of the process in Arizona, it could explain his erratic, changeable moods. She just didn't know what to believe anymore.

"This will sting," she warned, preparing to swab the wounds with antiseptic wash. She wasn't as gentle as she might've been and she took a bit too much glee in his shocked gasp. "Told you."

"You always do," he said through gritted teeth.

"Guess that's true." She'd often cleaned his scrapes and minor injuries on the days their mom was at work. "Some things don't change." But her brother had changed, in big and small ways she struggled to pin down.

She finished cleaning the wounds and pulled the gaps together with Steri-Strips and medical-grade superglue. While she might feel better if he had stitches, he was clearly opposed to the idea. "What's really going on, Trey?"

"I made some mistakes, all right?"

She bit back the immediate retort about dropping out of the college she'd worked so hard to pay for. "Have those mistakes put me in danger, too?"

"What?" His face paled and he lurched to his feet, putting the chair between them. "No. They just don't like it when people leave the program."

Obviously, the commune or cult or team Trey had joined was about far more than clean living, meditation and solar panels. Terri scooped up the remainder of his sleeve and folded it into the bloody washcloth and towel. "Following you all the way here seems a bit obsessive."

"Would you drop it?"

She'd been yelled at by patients before. The best response was none at all.

"Wait." Trey scrubbed at his face. "I'm sorry."

She continued cleaning up, wondering if he had any idea what a real apology was anymore. Moving as if he weren't even there, she repacked the first-aid kit, mopped up the blood and returned the chair to the table.

"Terri."

"Yes?" She paused to admire the flowers and flip through the mail.

"Thanks for cleaning me up."

"Sure."

"Come on!" His mood swung back to volatile, and he slammed a fist onto the counter. "You're worried about nothing. I handled it."

With her lips clamped together to restrain the lecture she wanted to deliver, she turned slowly to face him again. "Good. You'll want to keep that dry and rest your arm."

"You don't trust me," he stated.

"You're not giving me much reason to trust you." She pointed to the wounded arm. "I have no idea why you shot yourself, but you're damn lucky you didn't nick your brachial artery. You might've bled out before I got home."

"Shot myself?" he protested. "As if you'd care about anything more than the mess I'd leave behind."

Her hand fisted around the envelope she held, and it took all her self-control to keep that hand to herself. She wanted to slap him, to demand the truth. One honest answer could start rebuilding her trust.

Instead, she reached for her purse. She wouldn't stay here tonight. She couldn't. Arguing with her brother in this kitchen, bickering like children cast a pall over the house. The loving memories twisted into silent accusations as she realized her good intentions throughout his recovery had turned into something ugly and unhealthy. She didn't know how to fix it. She wasn't even sure it was hers to fix.

"Where are you going?" he asked.

"I can't stay here."

"I'll leave."

"It doesn't matter." She had to get out of this house. "That won't help. I need... I can't..." She swallowed. "I want you to be happy."

"Wait—"

Her cell phone rang, interrupting him. Thank God. She didn't want to hear more lies or excuses. She didn't know her brother anymore. The accident and grief had changed them both. Possibly beyond reconciliation. "It's the hospital," she said, checking the display before she answered. "This is Terri Barnhart."

"There's a crisis on the research ward," Franklin said, pain lancing his voice. "We need you immediately."

"I'm on my way." She left without a backward glance for her brother.

FROM HIS SURVEILLANCE position at the corner of the block, David watched Terri's car back out of the garage. Trey's motorcycle was still parked on the far side of the driveway. It irritated him how one call from her brother had put her on edge and amped up her frustration just when he'd managed to get her to relax. Confused, lost or discovering himself, Trey was someone David didn't trust. Too many answers didn't fit the big picture.

He told himself it was because Trey nearly

outed him with those bugs, but he wouldn't have been posted here with orders to keep Terri in his sights if there hadn't been a threat to begin with. David had barely cleared the driveway when Trey's motorcycle roared to life and he left a trail of rubber in the opposite direction. Good.

On a frustrated sigh, David called Trey's movements in to Casey's office. Before he could utter more than his name, Casey was on the line.

"Are you at the hospital?"

"No. I—"

"Get there. Dr. Palmer's sent an alert to his team about a problem with the patient."

That had to be what prompted Terri to leave the house so suddenly. She was too tenacious to give in or give up on an argument with her brother that quickly.

Casey said, "I have backup aimed your way, but they won't move without your signal."

"Excellent." It was a relief to know the best agents in the business were watching his back. "I'll call when I have something to report."

"I don't have to remind you how critical Palmer's advancements are. Protect the project at all costs."

"Yes, sir." David ended the call, hoping he wouldn't have to make a hard choice between Terri and the technology. Putting her second didn't feel right, despite his instincts to follow direct orders.

It didn't take him long to catch up with Terri. He kept driving when she turned into the employee parking area. Circling through the hospital campus, he looked for anyone or anything out of place. He cleared the immediate and obvious areas and parked in one of the reserved spaces near the front door. At this time of night he wasn't inconveniencing anyone.

The guard at the front desk disagreed. "You have to move that car, sir."

"Hey there," he said, flashing a smile along with his credentials. "A friend of mine called because of a scuffle on five." He came around to check the security cameras.

"No one told us about a problem," the guard replied. "You can't be back here."

"Only for a minute," David countered. "If you don't tell, I won't."

"Is this some kind of test?"

"Not at all. I'll be out of your hair in just a minute." He ignored the guard's opinion of his response as he watched the cameras covering Dr. Palmer's ward. "What's the latest access time on this ward?" He pointed.

The security guard grumbled as he double-checked the information. "I'm showing card swipes for Dr. Palmer and his nurse about two hours ago."

"Pull that up," he demanded. "Get me the visuals." The timing was impossible. Terri had been with him then. "Which nurse?"

"Barnhart."

A cold feeling settled in his gut. Keller had attacked. "Show me." He pulled out his phone to warn Terri away from the problem just as she walked into the real-time view of the camera.

Too late, he tapped the icon to call her. She swiped her card and the doors swung open. Given a choice between elevator and stairs, David opted for the stairwell. He would've lost his mind waiting for an elevator to show up.

He reached the fifth floor slightly winded and his quads burning. Cautious, he opened the stairwell door and peered into the hallway. The pervasive silence alarmed him. No murmur of voices, not a squeak of a shoe sole.

David looked right, where the double doors for the research wing were now closed. Terri and the patient were back there. The guard was gone. The bad feeling twisting David's stomach worsened.

He rolled his shoulders back and marched toward the closed doors. He swiped the one card that granted him access everywhere and waited for the light to turn green. It didn't. Before he could try again, he heard the unmistakable sound of a gun slide. The first bullet blew the security panel to hell and the second—or was it the third—plowed through his upper thigh as he ran for cover.

Where had the shooter come from? The feed had been live, and yet no one had spotted an armed man loitering on a secure floor? Had to be a setup, but who and why would have to wait.

David made it to the nurses station outside the lab, hoping to draw more attention away from Terri and Dr. Palmer on the other side of that door. As he reached for the security alarm under the desk, he took a blow to the back of the head. He shook it off, hit the alarm. He hoped Casey understood that the lights and siren were the signal. David swiveled, bracing his hips on the counter, and kicked his attacker in the stomach. No one he recognized.

The man came at him with a nasty black knife, and David groped for anything to use defensively. He came up with a keyboard. It worked, deflecting the man's aggressive attacks. The secure doors parted and someone shouted a command. Gunfire followed.

David knocked the man into the spray of bullets and threw himself over the high desk, more than happy to let the bad guys take each other out.

Alarms sounded and the lights in the corridor flashed in alternating red and white bursts. Stepping over the fallen man, David ignored the pain in his leg in an effort to get back to the secure door. His only thought was to help Terri.

The doors parted again and two more men emerged, shouting as they kept their guns trained on Terri. She was oblivious, her attention focused on a wounded man on the gurney. David struggled to breathe as his body slid down the wall. He had to protect her and the research patient. He moved—or thought he did—but the kidnappers were nearly to the end of the corridor. His vision blurred as blood dripped over his eye. He stared at his hand when it didn't do the expected thing and wipe the blood clear.

His other hand worked better and he cleaned his face. He had to get up. He looked toward the lights in the ceiling, telling himself it was like a dive that went a few minutes too long. Panic only made things worse. He slowed his breathing and reached for something to haul himself upright.

Terri needed him. Casey was counting on him. The woman, the research, the job all prodded him, but it wasn't enough to ward off the immediate injuries. He swore as the world went dark around him.

MINUTES OR HOURS LATER, he fought weakly against hands and winced at the bright lights as his vision returned. "Where am I?" he demanded through parched lips. "How long…"

"You're at MUSC. What day is it?"

"Friday. Right?"

"Right. That's a good sign."

He hissed as the man in the ER uniform pressed something cold to his forehead. "You took a nasty blow."

"I'm fine," David said. "Ryan," he added, squinting at the name embroidered over the pocket. "How long have I been out?"

"Hard to say. You've been shot," Ryan said. "Hold still."

"I know. Slap a bandage on my leg and let me up."

"You need—"

"To save Terri and Palmer," David said, cutting him off again. "I'm good. Help me up."

Ryan ignored him. "A doctor should look at this."

"Later." He had to pick up the trail or… He couldn't even think about the consequences for Terri, Palmer, the project or himself if he failed.

"Leave the heroics to someone else," Ryan said. "We've called the police."

"I am the someone else," David argued. He sucked in a breath as Ryan poured something over the gash in his leg. "What do you know about the situation?"

"Yours or in general?"

"Come on, man."

"All I know is bad guys and guns showed up in the hospital, killed a patient and kidnapped a nurse and doctor. And nearly killed you. Security is trying to figure out how weapons got in here at all."

"I have to go after them." He coughed, tasting the copper tang of blood in his mouth. "Have to find the trail."

"That would be against any logical medical advice." Ryan stood and offered David his hand.

He hated the assist, but it was better than making a fool of himself. For a second it was like those first hours on a ship with the deck swaying underfoot, and then his senses stabilized. He didn't have time for injuries; Terri needed him now. If he lost her, if he failed the case... Well, there was no point in wasting time thinking negatively.

No game, no dive, no operation was over until he'd won. This would not be the exception. He'd come too far with Terri, as well as the case.

He stalked into the secure ward and joined the others gathered around the violent remains of a fight and Dr. Palmer's dead research patient. "Do we know anything about the attackers?"

"Domestic terrorist is the theory, but that's about it."

David bit back the curse. He couldn't waste any more time. Turning on his heel, he moved as fast as his injuries allowed, following the trail of blood on the hospital floor.

Chapter Fourteen

Terri struggled to maintain pressure on Franklin's wound as the kidnappers shoved them into the back of an ambulance. Images, disjointed and nonsensical, flashed through her mind. Blood on the linens and floor. Blood on the wheels of the gurney. The sharp blast of gunfire and the burning smell in the air afterward. Matt limp in the bed. David fighting in the corridor only to fall, bleeding, against the window in the hallway. What had he been doing there?

Her one regret as she worked on Franklin was not telling David her real feelings. She loved him. Would she soon die with all that wonderful and scary emotion bottled up inside her? It hardly mattered if David was already dead.

Had she called his name? She'd stayed with Franklin, had to as the terrorists made dire threats and her hands were all that had stemmed the flow of blood. But she'd wanted to help David. Had he reached for her? She couldn't remember. Too strange. She pushed the terrible unknowns away and gave Franklin her full attention.

"If he dies, you die," the man said, slamming the ambulance doors shut. She shivered. In Matt's room, the others had called the man Joe and treated him like the leader. His eyes were colder than his brutal words and she had no doubt this was the man Trey blamed for his injury. She shuddered with disgust and fear. Neither she nor Franklin would live long after these men got what they were after.

The siren blared and the ambulance swayed side to side as the driver swerved in and out of traffic. She didn't know where they were going, only that she had to keep pressure on Franklin's wound. What had happened to Trey? She added another layer of gauze to the stack covering the ragged bullet hole just above Franklin's hipbone. She kept her eyes open. Closing them brought back the images of David collapsing.

She hoped her brother had done the right thing and called the police. He'd been reluctant, but at this rate, she couldn't see how things could get any worse. Franklin needed more medical attention than she could give. Her mind raced through an anatomy diagram and she tried to stay calm as she assessed the amount of blood loss. One step at a time.

"I can stabilize you," she said with more conviction than she felt. Her emotions would wait. Worry had no place during the triage process. Stop the bleeding. Prevent shock. Start an IV. Administer pain meds. She'd heard it all, assisted many a doctor through the process. This wasn't a lost cause—she wouldn't let it be—but more hands would help. She pressed Franklin's hand over the gauze. "Hold this."

Franklin shook his head. "Forget me," he rasped, pain contorting his features. "Escape."

Terri shook her head. "Not without you."

"It's too late for me. The work… It's over. My research is done."

She heard what he left unsaid. The last of his family was gone. Murdered. Why was life so cruel? She clenched her jaw, her heart breaking for her friend. She'd known this raw, wrenching loss. First his daughter and now his son-in-law killed by horrible, selfish men. Only men who didn't value life could believe death was a fair price for advancing a cause. Franklin's world would never be the same, but she wouldn't let him give up. They still had each other.

"The good guys need you," she murmured at his ear. "Don't you dare let these bastards win."

"Shut up!" Joe bellowed from the front seat.

Terri sent him a fuming glare as a fiery determination blazed to life inside her. If Franklin had to hang on, so would she. She refused to become an easy target. "Speaking to a patient is helpful," she said in the authoritative voice she used in the ER with panicked patients or families. "You can help or you can stay out of it."

The creep shook his head and swore at her, but he faced forward.

"Go." Franklin weakly pushed at her shoulder. "Save yourself."

"Stop it." Terri would never be able to bear it if she left him alone to die with these monsters. "To hell with work or research. *I* need you."

Her brother had betrayed her trust one too many times. She'd always love him, but his warped, selfish view of the world meant she had to keep her distance. Besides whatever she and David might have, Franklin was the only person she had left. He'd been father and friend, a good listener and a compassionate, generous employer.

"David—" Franklin coughed. "David will find me."

Her stomach clutched and icy fingers danced down her spine. She trembled. "Of course," she lied, grieving over Franklin's obvious confusion. It didn't make sense to her that Franklin expected help from David, but if the image gave him comfort, she wouldn't tell Franklin she'd left David injured, possibly dead, in a hospital hallway. She wouldn't steal his hope that way.

"Then he'll find us," she agreed. Her heart fluttered as if Franklin's hope had kindled her own. She ignored it, getting back to practical matters. "Stop wasting energy arguing with me. You know I'm right."

His only reply was another weak cough.

She reached for the emergency supplies she would need. The ambulance barreled around a corner, and the back end bounced as the tires went over the curb. "Take it easy," she shouted. "I'm trying to save a man's life here."

"Shut up!"

With the bastards up front focused on fleeing, she tucked anything sharp she could get her hands on into her pockets, as well as Franklin's. She intended to make the most of any possible opportunity to impede the kidnappers.

By the time the ambulance came to a stop, she had the needle in Franklin's vein and had started the IV. She added morphine, far less than he needed, but she'd never get him out of here if he was incapacitated. Neither man in the front seat moved.

The back doors suddenly opened. Her brother stood there, looking as dumbstruck as she felt. "Trey?"

He turned to the man behind him. "Let her go."

"Not my call." He pushed Trey hard enough to send him sprawling into the ambulance.

"Move!" Joe said from the front seat. "Our ride won't wait forever."

"What's going on?" she demanded when Trey and the third man were squeezed into the space.

Trey shook his head. "I'm sorry."

Now she got a real apology? "Oh, you will be," she vowed. With the guard's eyes watching her every move, she tended to Franklin, refusing to make eye contact with her brother or the guard.

"I can get you out."

The guard snorted, and she felt herself agreeing with the stranger over her brother. "Don't grow a conscience on my account," she grumbled. "It's likely to get you hurt worse, and I have my hands full as it is keeping Franklin alive."

"You just stay put," the guard said to Trey. "Don't let that man die," he told Terri, nodding to Franklin.

Her patience snapped. "You do realize his best chance of survival is a trauma center? I'm partial to MUSC, of course."

"What do you need?"

She gawked at the guard. "A staffed operating room." She let the tears well in her eyes. If he underestimated her, maybe it would give her a chance. "This gauze and IV are stopgaps at best." With a sniffle, she checked Franklin's vitals. "Not that it matters."

"It matters," Trey said. The guard drove the butt of his gun into Trey's side, stealing his air.

"I suggest you get creative," the guard said. "Joe doesn't cope well with disappointment."

The ambulance stopped short, and this time both the driver and Joe leaped from the front seat. When the back doors opened, she realized they'd reached the city marina. The guard and Trey were tasked with moving Franklin's stretcher. Terri had her hands full carrying all the gear she could manage. She wasn't about to leave behind anything valuable as a weapon or helpful to Franklin.

"Why didn't the police follow us?" she wondered aloud. Charleston was small enough, and the hospital was close to the harbor. All the driving they'd done made no sense.

"They sent out a decoy at the same time," Trey explained.

"Shut up!" Joe bellowed as they moved down the dock.

"You're drawing attention to yourself," she said in the calm voice that seemed to annoy him. If she could force him to make another mistake or outburst, surely someone out here would report a disturbance. Barring that, she had to find a way to leave behind something that would get reported. Joe and the driver were ahead of her.

Trey and the third guard were behind her. What could she spare that wouldn't get lost or noticed?

She wrestled with her stethoscope and knocked loose a few pads of bloody gauze at the same time. It was a paltry attempt and it would likely fail, but it was her only option. Anything else would surely be noticed.

Joe led the way onto a large cabin cruiser and ordered Terri, Trey and Franklin down below and out of sight.

When they were alone, she checked Franklin's blood pressure and pulse. He didn't have much longer.

"Will he make it?" Trey asked.

Didn't he understand anything? She turned her back on Franklin and shot her brother a dark look. Her voice was upbeat when she replied, "Of course."

Trey shuffled his feet, crossing and uncrossing his arms, then rubbing his hands together. "I need to do something," Trey whispered.

"Make it the right something this time," she snapped. "Adding to your mistakes won't help any of us."

She opened the bag of supplies and started to clean the gore from her friend's hands. It seemed they'd stemmed the worst of the bleeding, but they needed to get that bullet out of his hip.

"We have to do something," Trey said, peering out of the porthole.

"We will." Terri wanted to scream at Trey's impatience. Understanding carried her only so far. If he didn't man up and show some sign of responsible behavior in this crisis, she might knock him out just for her own peace of mind. "What were you thinking, falling in with Joe and his friends?"

Trey's mouth flatlined in defiance for a moment. Then his shoulders fell and he slumped onto the nearest bunk. "I didn't mean to drop out of college," he confessed. "It did start with an interest rally on campus."

"Terrorism 101?"

Trey shook his head. "It was a health and wholeness thing. It was a time suck, but I felt good in the sessions. Strong," he said, raising his head and meeting her gaze.

The sorrow almost undid her. She wanted to go to him, to wrap her arms around him and tell him it would be fine, but she'd done that before. This time he'd have to find his own way out.

A deep rumble rattled through the boat. "Oh, crap," Trey said. "The engines."

Terri's heart sank as their options dwindled. "Where would Joe take us?"

"How should I know?"

She wanted to throttle him. "Think, Trey. This

team sucked you in to get to Franklin. Where would they take a doctor researching biotech devices?"

"Biotech?"

He sounded surprised. Too surprised. She studied him like a virus under a microscope. He might've been getting tan and fit in the desert, but those few months couldn't erase a lifetime of habits. She stepped away from Franklin, weaving a bit as the boat gained speed. "What do you know?"

"Nothing, Terri. I was just in the wrong place at the wrong time."

"You're lying," she stated baldly. "We're on a boat with at least one terrorist and the man who helped me fund your college tuition is dying." She flung an arm in Franklin's direction.

"I'll get us out of this," Trey said. "I just need a few minutes with Joe."

"And you'll bargain with what? Franklin's life?"

"I won't let you get hurt." He grabbed her shoulders. "I swear you were never supposed to be this close to the action."

She knocked his arms away and rushed back to Franklin's side. "If you had any sway over your friends, you wouldn't be locked in here with me."

"I'm locked up with you because they know I turned them in."

"Oh, right."

"It's the truth!" he shouted.

Franklin startled at Trey's outburst and she soothed him. "I don't care whose side you think you're on now," she said, keeping her voice even in deference to Franklin's condition. "I won't let you use Franklin."

"Terri, be reasonable."

She laughed, the sound bitter in her ears. "What has that ever got me with you?" She looked at Franklin. His skin pasty and clammy, she knew she had to do something or he wouldn't make it. "You want reasonable?"

Her brother nodded.

"You want to do something helpful?"

Another nod.

She pulled on latex gloves and threw the box at him. "Help me save his life."

Now Trey paled under his tan. "What do you mean?"

"He took a bullet meant for me when your pals killed his son-in-law. You can start by helping me get it out of him."

"Terri, I can't."

"You can." Her temper snapped. "You will. Put on the gloves. If he dies, they kill me, too."

She cut him off when he would've protested.

"Without this man we wouldn't have made it those first months after Dad and Mom died. If you won't do it for me, or your self-respect, for God's sake do it to honor the way you were raised."

She wouldn't compound that tragedy by losing Franklin, too.

"You can't operate here," Trey protested as he snapped on the latex gloves.

"Then you'll have a chance to prove your influence when I fail." She checked the straps securing Franklin to the gurney and refused to let Trey's doubts creep into her head. Was this ideal? Not even close, but she had to try and get that bullet out and repair the damage it had done.

She set to work, her hands busy with the task in front of her while her heart prayed.

DAVID, HIS LEG bandaged under his torn pants, fought off the queasiness that went along with his certain concussion as he made his way to the first of two dark SUVs crowding the street corner. There would be time to recover once Terri and Dr. Palmer were safe.

Police had been called in and a search was under way for the ambulance Keller's team had used as a getaway vehicle. Anxiety turned his palms damp. This strike had been swift and well organized. He keenly felt every second that carried Terri farther from his reach.

The back door opened, and David climbed in to sit beside Director Casey. "Thanks for bringing the cavalry," he said. "You're caught up on the mess inside?" He tipped his head back toward the hospital.

"We are," Casey replied. "I only wish we'd been closer when we learned what was going down."

"I put a transmitter on her badge," David said, giving the frequency to his friend Noah Drake, who sat in the front seat with a laptop.

It felt like an eternity before the positive response came back. "Got it." Another long pause. "Either the badge has been discarded and they've tossed her in the harbor, or they're on a boat. Rate of movement suggests boat."

Small consolation. David leaned around the seat to study the screen. "I can get them out." Despite his fuzzy head, he would breach any watercraft to make this rescue. The world needed Dr. Palmer and he needed Terri.

"Is Palmer with her?" Casey asked.

David eyed his boss. "He is."

Casey's face was grave. "We have to reach them before it's too late."

"If they're on the water I can get them out. You know I can get them out."

Noah gave more stats on the transmitter.

"There's no time to call in other water experts," David said. He was begging now and didn't care.

"There's the Coast Guard," Casey reminded him.

"Great, they can back me up when they get here. Franklin will need medical attention based on the way Terri was working on him."

"You're injured."

David shrugged off the concern. His injuries didn't matter. Terri mattered. Dr. Palmer's work mattered. "Where's Trey? He left her house shortly after she was called to the hospital." David wished he'd taken the chance and found a way to tag Trey.

"We don't know about Trey."

"Give me the heading," he said. "If they're in open water, the Coast Guard can intercept," he said to Casey. "If not…"

He let it hang out there as he debated the limited options. A boat, dive gear and a weapon. According to the intel, the Keller strike team totaled five, and one of them was in custody already. David considered Trey neutral, especially if Keller had hurt Terri. Which left the odds at one against three. He could manage that.

"I know every inch of this coastline," David urged. "Let me get after them. I can do this."

Casey's nod was barely visible in the shadows. The driver put the SUV in gear and aimed for the City Marina as David barked out the items he needed before anyone could change the director's mind.

In record time, proving Casey had anticipated yet another contingency, David had a small tactical strike boat ready to launch. Following the transmitter signal, with Noah as backup, he zipped across the dark water of the Charleston harbor.

"Looks like they're headed for Fort Sumter," Noah reported while David gently shifted the rudder accordingly. "I'll call it in."

David goosed the engine. It galled him that they'd abuse a national monument for their own agenda. Much as he loved the good work of his Coast Guard, he wanted to get there first. He needed to know Terri was safe, not hear it secondhand. As for Trey and the bastards who'd turned him into a criminal, that problem was one he'd happily let the authorities work out.

Keller's boat was running dark. The engine on the strike boat was designed to run quieter, and David kept the noise under that of the bigger vessel. He hugged the shallow area, angling between the shore and Keller's boat. If they wanted to get on that island, they'd have to go through him.

"David?"

He heard the warning in Noah's voice. "I want to handle this on open water. What does infrared show?"

"One in the stern near the engine, two amidships and three in the aft cabin."

"Got it." That would be Terri, Trey and Franklin in the cabin, and that was all that mattered. The rest was just minor detail work.

"Coast Guard is five minutes away," Noah added.

"Then I'll be quick." He positioned the strike boat just off the cruiser's port bow, running practically within arm's reach. A sharp crew on the bigger boat would have heard them and they'd be taking fire. David accepted the luck that gave him the small advantage here. This team had done enough damage at the hospital. He slid between the boats, and the shock of the cold water closing over him cleared his head. The resulting sense of calm honed his determination. His leg ached less as he bobbed for a few seconds before catching the cruiser's bumper.

He thought of the infrared signals and the transmitters as he hauled his body up to the low deck of the stern.

The man standing guard was gazing toward the approaching island. David knocked him out with a blow to the back of his head and noiselessly lowered him to the deck.

Taking the man's gun, David ignored his twinging leg as he examined the surroundings for his next target. Keller was at the wheel with another man at his side.

They were closing in on the Fort Sumter dock. Although he didn't know what Keller had planned, he wouldn't risk letting him off this boat.

Weighing his options and the backup en route, David leaned over and fired several rounds into the outboard motors. Once the cabin cruiser's engines died, the strike boat's engine sounded like a deafening roar out here.

As the boat drifted, Keller grabbed his gun and squeezed off random bursts over the side in the direction of the strike boat. Noah fired a warning volley and demanded Joe's surrender.

Knowing Noah could handle himself, David used the distraction to head to the cabin. He had to get to Terri before Keller could use her or Franklin as bargaining chips. A beam of light swept across the cruiser's deck, and a voice on loudspeaker, demanding cooperation, filled the darkness.

The Coast Guard had arrived.

David hurried forward to take care of the guard covering Terri and Dr. Palmer. But the door opened and he faced Trey. David didn't want to hurt him, but he wouldn't allow the brother to keep hurting Terri, either.

"Whose side are you on?"

"Terri's," Trey answered immediately, holding up his hands. "We heard shots and the engines die and I want to help."

"Get up on deck," David ordered. "Cooperate with the authorities."

Trey bobbed his head and squeezed past David to the deck. David didn't move until he was sure Trey was behaving. Then he entered the cabin.

Terri stood over Franklin, her face flushed and her scrubs smeared with his blood. "David! Thank God, you're alive."

Her smile was the most beautiful sight in the world. "You, too," he said as relief overcame him. "How's your patient?"

"Stable at last. He needs a surgeon."

"We can manage that." He wanted to hold her, to confess every emotion pounding through him. "You're not hurt?"

She shook her head. "I thought you…were dead." A tear rolled down her cheek.

He limped closer, unable to stand even the smallest distance any longer. He was at a loss for words. All he could do was hold her and savor the touch as she wrapped her arms around him.

The boarding party filled the cabin like a rush

of the tide and then disappeared with equal efficiency as they transferred Franklin to the helicopter standing by to take him to MUSC.

Chapter Fifteen

Saturday, December 14, 6:10 a.m.

The sun was a glowing hint on the horizon when David finally had a chance to draw Terri away from the chaos. They'd returned Keller's boat to the marina and relinquished control of the vessel to the Coast Guard. At that point they had been tugged in opposite directions for questioning and treatment.

"Come sit with me?" he asked, taking her hand and leading her to a quiet bench close to the water. "You're a hero, sweetheart. Saving Dr. Palmer was crucial to the ongoing efforts against terrorism. Whatever Trey did will get sorted out. I hear he's in a cooperative mood."

"It's about time. He used my access card to hurt people."

The pain in her voice tore at him. David had to make her understand that as bad as things looked right now it would get better. He wanted this to mark a new beginning. For her and her brother—and for the two of them.

That meant coming clean about his role in all of this and coping with her decisions about him personally.

He pushed a hand through his hair. "Your brother wasn't exactly wrong about me," David said. He could see by the way her face fell that he was already screwing this up. "I'm not a spy," he added quickly, "but I was sent here as an operative for a specific purpose."

TERRI GAZED OUT over the horizon. They had to have this conversation, and sooner was better than later. "So I was…" She swallowed, waved a finger between them. "This, um, you and me. It was some kind of assignment?"

She thought of her brother and realized the enormous consequences of his mistakes were going to spill over onto her, too, in more ways than one. This kind of security breach could end her career as a nurse. The security team in charge of Franklin's research had been right about the risk she'd posed. She had been too blinded by love for Trey to see it.

"No," David replied emphatically. He gave her shoulders a squeeze, then brought her hands to his lips and kissed her knuckles. "I was assigned to Charleston for a reason. My role to provide intel and perspective and to be on hand in the case of a terrorist attack hasn't changed."

"Hasn't it?" All the flashing lights made her feel as if she'd walked into a grotesque mockery of holiday displays. It looked as though his assignment was over to her.

"No. Terri, look at me." He tipped up her chin.

Twenty-four hours ago, the move would've made her smile as she eagerly anticipated the glorious sensation of his mouth on hers. Now she stared into those gray depths, simply amazed he was alive. She'd cling to that, be grateful he'd survived even though their time as friends and lovers was over.

"My assignment hasn't changed."

She felt the tears welling. If that was true, then there was no hope for them. After this debacle she'd never pass another security interview. A blast of fury shot through her veins. It wasn't fair that Trey's misplaced loyalty could ruin everything for her. The anger faded almost as quickly as it had arrived. Life wasn't fair and happy endings were for fairy tales. She would manage. That was what she did. She'd start over from scratch somewhere far away.

"Are you listening?"

She nodded.

"You are not." He pressed his mouth to hers and she was no match for the tenderness. He leaned back and brushed the tear off her cheek. "They're leaving me posted here."

"Good. You like Charleston." She'd watched him fall in love with the area, knew being close to his family was important to him.

Family. Merely thinking the word had a new wave of tears threatening to further humiliate her. Director Casey had told her that Trey and Franklin would be in isolation and protective custody while the authorities tracked down the men Joe Keller reported to for this attack. No one seemed to know how long that would take. He'd offered her a protective detail, but she'd passed.

She had to leave. There wouldn't be a place for her here anymore. Not a place that didn't remind her of loss and pain.

She leaned back, away from David's warm, soothing touch. As much as she wanted to burrow into the comfort he offered, a clean break was better than drawing this out. "Thank you," she said, pausing to catch her breath. "For saving Franklin and me. And Trey."

"Terri—"

"I get it." She wished she could muster a smile. "Really. I'll find something else, somewhere else to be." Too bad she didn't have any idea where to start.

"Terri." He gave her shoulders a gentle shake. "I like Charleston, but I love *you*."

"Pardon?" He couldn't have said what she thought she'd heard.

"Do I have your attention now?"

Her head felt loose on her neck as she nodded this time. "I need to sit down."

"You are sitting down." David chuckled as he patted her leg and she trembled. He wrapped his arm around her shoulders.

Words were impossible. Even the ones she wanted to say. Breathing was enough of a challenge. "It's… I…"

"It wasn't that serious for you? If we're not on the same page, that's okay."

She thought they might be closer than she'd dared to hope. "Won't keeping me around be problematic for you?"

"I told you this won't blow back on you."

"Because of your connections?"

"Because you're a hero."

That word again. It felt too big and described him far better. She shook her head. "That's not me. I'd be dead by now if you hadn't found us."

"Let's forget the circumstances for a minute," he said. "Fact is, we're good together, however we met. We're an excellent team. I want you in my life. For the rest of my life."

The words were so sweet, delivered in the

Southern accent that had her believing dreams could come true. Even the one where they lived happily ever after.

"You make an excellent shark steak."

He leaned back and gave her a quizzical look. "I can't remember if I told you that before my brother's call interrupted us."

"The way I remember it, we were working on dessert when he called."

"No." The friendly banter eased the tension. "I was working my way up to telling you I was in love with you. It's been really hard to hold it back."

"You don't ever need to hold anything back with me."

"I feel the same way," she said, leaning close for a sweet kiss.

"I don't want to give up what we've started, but I don't want to hurt your career or cover or whatever," she murmured, her gaze fixed on the harbor.

"You can't." He rubbed his hand up and down her arm. "My cover only gets stronger with you in it."

"How is that possible?"

He smiled. "We're the great love story at the hospital. The rumors are something about me, the HR desk jockey, being propelled by love to jump into the fray and chase down the kidnappers with the help of my old Coast Guard pals. The truth can be surprisingly effective."

She wanted to laugh but couldn't quite manage it. "You don't find that a little like a romance novel?"

"I don't care. Nothing else matters. I meant what I said about wanting you for the rest of my days." He eased back from her. "Unless, of course, you aren't interested in something long-term."

She scooted closer, more than interested in something long-term with him. If only it didn't feel rather impossible. "I made mistakes—"

"You were innocent, Terri," he insisted. "Trust me, the people who know the facts will make sure the blame lands on the right people."

"My brother being one of them."

"His decisions are his own, Terri."

"I know." Sadness and betrayal were a strange mix inside her. People had died because of Trey's bad choices. As much as she wanted to be there for him, to support him while he dealt with the emotional and legal consequences, she couldn't put her life on hold any longer.

"As are yours."

"I know," she repeated.

She thought of Matt and his unflagging determination to avenge and honor his wife. Their time together had been short, but the love had been true. She thought of her parents, of how they'd been together, full of life and love through good times and bad. They'd made decisions that empowered their children, and their devotion to each other had been something she'd longed to bring into her life. She'd just been waiting for the right man.

For David, she realized as an invisible weight lifted from her shoulders. "I choose us," she said, linking her hand with his. The words felt right. Comfortable. Her heart swelled in her chest with the miracle of hope and happiness. "I want to be a part of your life. No matter what comes our way, we can tackle it together."

David stood, bringing her along and pulling her body against his. His lips brushed hers in a tender reprise of their first kiss on her porch. She looped her arms around his neck and kissed him back, forgetting the rest of the world amid the simple perfection of the moment.

"My parents would have adored you," she said, pausing to catch her breath. David was her present and her future. He was the anchor who would keep her from getting lost in the tempest of her past or whatever came their way in the future.

"I'm glad." He rested his forehead against hers. "My family will be head over heels when they meet you. I hope their exuberance doesn't scare you off."

"Not a chance," she promised, tiptoeing to kiss him again. "Beside you, I feel downright invincible."

"Together we are, I'm sure of it," he replied.

She wrapped her arms around his waist and snuggled into the shelter of his embrace, his heart beating under her cheek as they watched the sun rise, filling the first day of their lives together with light and genuine happiness.

Epilogue

Thomas stood at his office window, not seeing anything but the reflection of his past. He felt a small sting of guilt removing some of his best people from the Specialist team. It couldn't be helped. Dangers and threats cropped up every day, targeting innocent people and valuable assets.

For a moment he wondered if he'd been given this assignment just so he couldn't retire. He was either too close to the situation or too jaded to see a place where he could call it done.

"Are you ready?"

Thomas turned to find his wife, Jo, waiting for him in the open doorway, right on time for their dinner date. She was the light at the end of the tunnel, the ray of hope that kept him moving through those résumés so he could walk away in good conscience.

Soon, his successor would take over this office and the burdens that went along with it. Thomas shrugged into his coat, smiling as he crossed the office to kiss his wife.

He turned out the light and locked his door. Tomorrow was soon enough to resume his search to match the best operatives with the highest threat risks inside America's borders. He wouldn't rest until he had posted heroes next door to wherever they were needed.

* * * * *

LARGER-PRINT BOOKS!

HARLEQUIN

Presents®

GET 2 FREE LARGER-PRINT NOVELS PLUS 2 FREE GIFTS!

PASSION GUARANTEED SEDUCTION

YES! Please send me 2 FREE LARGER-PRINT Harlequin Presents® novels and my 2 FREE gifts (gifts are worth about $10). After receiving them, if I don't wish to receive any more books, I can return the shipping statement marked "cancel." If I don't cancel, I will receive 6 brand-new novels every month and be billed just $5.30 per book in the U.S. or $5.74 per book in Canada. That's a saving of at least 12% off the cover price! It's quite a bargain! Shipping and handling is just 50¢ per book in the U.S. and 75¢ per book in Canada.* I understand that accepting the 2 free books and gifts places me under no obligation to buy anything. I can always return a shipment and cancel at any time. Even if I never buy another book, the two free books and gifts are mine to keep forever.

176/376 HDN GHVY

Name _____ (PLEASE PRINT)

Address _____ Apt. #

City _____ State/Prov. _____ Zip/Postal Code

Signature (if under 18, a parent or guardian must sign)

Mail to the **Reader Service:**
IN U.S.A.: P.O. Box 1867, Buffalo, NY 14240-1867
IN CANADA: P.O. Box 609, Fort Erie, Ontario L2A 5X3

**Are you a subscriber to Harlequin Presents® books
and want to receive the larger-print edition?
Call 1-800-873-8635 today or visit us at www.ReaderService.com.**

* Terms and prices subject to change without notice. Prices do not include applicable taxes. Sales tax applicable in N.Y. Canadian residents will be charged applicable taxes. Offer not valid in Quebec. This offer is limited to one order per household. Not valid for current subscribers to Harlequin Presents Larger-Print books. All orders subject to credit approval. Credit or debit balances in a customer's account(s) may be offset by any other outstanding balance owed by or to the customer. Please allow 4 to 6 weeks for delivery. Offer available while quantities last.

Your Privacy—The Reader Service is committed to protecting your privacy. Our Privacy Policy is available online at www.ReaderService.com or upon request from the Reader Service.

We make a portion of our mailing list available to reputable third parties that offer products we believe may interest you. If you prefer that we not exchange your name with third parties, or if you wish to clarify or modify your communication preferences, please visit us at www.ReaderService.com/consumerchoice or write to us at Reader Service Preference Service, P.O. Box 9062, Buffalo, NY 14240-9062. Include your complete name and address.

HPLP15

LARGER-PRINT BOOKS!
GET 2 FREE LARGER-PRINT NOVELS PLUS
2 FREE GIFTS!

HARLEQUIN®

Romance

From the Heart, For the Heart

YES! Please send me 2 FREE LARGER-PRINT Harlequin® Romance novels and my 2 FREE gifts (gifts are worth about $10). After receiving them, if I don't wish to receive any more books, I can return the shipping statement marked "cancel." If I don't cancel, I will receive 4 brand-new novels every month and be billed just $5.09 per book in the U.S. or $5.49 per book in Canada. That's a savings of at least 15% off the cover price! It's quite a bargain! Shipping and handling is just 50¢ per book in the U.S. and 75¢ per book in Canada.* I understand that accepting the 2 free books and gifts places me under no obligation to buy anything. I can always return a shipment and cancel at any time. Even if I never buy another book, the two free books and gifts are mine to keep forever.

119/319 HDN GHWC

Name	(PLEASE PRINT)	

Address		Apt. #

City	State/Prov.	Zip/Postal Code

Signature (if under 18, a parent or guardian must sign)

Mail to the Reader Service:
IN U.S.A.: P.O. Box 1867, Buffalo, NY 14240-1867
IN CANADA: P.O. Box 609, Fort Erie, Ontario L2A 5X3
Want to try two free books from another line?
Call 1-800-873-8635 or visit www.ReaderService.com.

* Terms and prices subject to change without notice. Prices do not include applicable taxes. Sales tax applicable in N.Y. Canadian residents will be charged applicable taxes. Offer not valid in Quebec. This offer is limited to one order per household. Not valid for current subscribers to Harlequin Romance Larger-Print books. All orders subject to credit approval. Credit or debit balances in a customer's account(s) may be offset by any other outstanding balance owed by or to the customer. Please allow 4 to 6 weeks for delivery. Offer available while quantities last.

Your Privacy—The Reader Service is committed to protecting your privacy. Our Privacy Policy is available online at www.ReaderService.com or upon request from the Reader Service.

We make a portion of our mailing list available to reputable third parties that offer products we believe may interest you. If you prefer that we not exchange your name with third parties, or if you wish to clarify or modify your communication preferences, please visit us at www.ReaderService.com/consumerchoice or write to us at Reader Service Preference Service, P.O. Box 9062, Buffalo, NY 14240-9062. Include your complete name and address.

HRLP15

LARGER-PRINT BOOKS!
GET 2 FREE LARGER-PRINT NOVELS PLUS
2 FREE GIFTS!

HARLEQUIN

super romance

More Story...More Romance

YES! Please send me 2 FREE LARGER-PRINT Harlequin® Superromance® novels and my 2 FREE gifts (gifts are worth about $10). After receiving them, if I don't wish to receive any more books, I can return the shipping statement marked "cancel." If I don't cancel, I will receive 4 brand-new novels every month and be billed just $5.94 per book in the U.S. or $6.24 per book in Canada. That's a savings of at least 12% off the cover price! It's quite a bargain! Shipping and handling is just 50¢ per book in the U.S. or 75¢ per book in Canada.* I understand that accepting the 2 free books and gifts places me under no obligation to buy anything. I can always return a shipment and cancel at any time. Even if I never buy another book, the two free books and gifts are mine to keep forever.

132/332 HDN GHVC

Name _____ (PLEASE PRINT)

Address _____ Apt. #

City _____ State/Prov. _____ Zip/Postal Code

Signature (if under 18, a parent or guardian must sign)

Mail to the Reader Service:
IN U.S.A.: P.O. Box 1867, Buffalo, NY 14240-1867
IN CANADA: P.O. Box 609, Fort Erie, Ontario L2A 5X3

Want to try two free books from another line?
Call 1-800-873-8635 today or visit www.ReaderService.com.

* Terms and prices subject to change without notice. Prices do not include applicable taxes. Sales tax applicable in N.Y. Canadian residents will be charged applicable taxes. Offer not valid in Quebec. This offer is limited to one order per household. Not valid for current subscribers to Harlequin Superromance Larger-Print books. All orders subject to credit approval. Credit or debit balances in a customer's account(s) may be offset by any other outstanding balance owed by or to the customer. Please allow 4 to 6 weeks for delivery. Offer available while quantities last.

Your Privacy—The Reader Service is committed to protecting your privacy. Our Privacy Policy is available online at www.ReaderService.com or upon request from the Reader Service.

We make a portion of our mailing list available to reputable third parties that offer products we believe may interest you. If you prefer that we not exchange your name with third parties, or if you wish to clarify or modify your communication preferences, please visit us at www.ReaderService.com/consumerschoice or write to us at Reader Service Preference Service, P.O. Box 9062, Buffalo, NY 14240-9062. Include your complete name and address.

HSRLP15

READERSERVICE.COM

Manage your account online!

- Review your order history
- Manage your payments
- Update your address

*We've designed the
Reader Service website
just for you.*

Enjoy all the features!

- Discover new series available to you, and read excerpts from any series.
- Respond to mailings and special monthly offers.
- Connect with favorite authors at the blog.
- Browse the Bonus Bucks catalog and online-only exculsives.
- Share your feedback.

Visit us at:
ReaderService.com

RS15